AF409069

BLACK CEASAR

AD Eaton
Black Ceasar

All rights reserved
Copyright © 2023 by AD Eaton

No part of this publication may be reproduced, distributed, or
transmitted in any form or by any means, including photocopying,
recording, or other electronic or mechanical methods, without the
prior written permission of the publisher, except in the case of brief
quotations embodied in critical reviews and certain other
noncommercial uses permitted by copyright law.

Published by BooxAI
ISBN: 978-965-578-710-8

BLACK CEASAR

AD EATON

CONTENTS

ACKNOWLEDGMENTS

First, I would like to thank God for providing me with a gift to be able to use my words and bring stories to life.

Never in a million years have I thought I would be motivating others to change their lives based on the words that I put in a book.

I would also like to thank my wonderful wife and children for being all the push that I needed to keep writing and pursuing my dreams.

To my father, who put countless hours in to ensure that this project was finished in time…and to anyone who may not have the actual dollar yet does have the magic of a dream, all it takes is a spark to light that flame. Again, I say to you all… THANKS.

DEDICATION

I would like to dedicate this book to my family and closest friends for motivating me to complete what I started. It all started with a vision to be able to tell the unheard stories that are still relevant to our current state in society. Not everyone has the resources to be able to tell their story, so this is me giving them a voice.

1

BLACK CEASAR

Ring
Ring
Ring

Ceasar's phone rings for a third time, waking both he and Tory out of their sleep.

"Hello!" Ceasar answered angrily.

"Bro, my bad," Deon says, "I know you sleep, but I need that ASAP. I was supposed to have been on the road at five this morning... it's already six now."

"Nigga, if you would have pulled up on me last night, we wouldn't be having this problem."

Deon could see that Ceasar was growing irritated but continued to push anyway...

"Come on, Ceaz, you know for yourself that I need to make this play, mane... and Keon is already down there with everybody on standby. All you gotta do is blow the horn when you pull up, and the rest is handled. "

Ceasar looked over at Tory, still asleep with her mouth halfway open.

"Aight... give me 45 minutes," he said, giving in.

Deon answers and replies anxiously, "Bet..." and hangs up the phone.

All he's thinking about now is how much money he's looking at making off of this trip.

Ceasar slides his arm out from under Tory while actually trying to sneak out of bed.

"Unh-unh...," Tory moans, "Nigga, where you think you are going this early in the morning without giving me my *wake and bake?*"

"The only *wake and bake* that's on the menu this early in the *am* is DICK baby," Ceasar answers before going on, " I got somewhere to be in the next hour. But... if you hurry up, I can show you what that *roll-over* dick is like."

Tory slides her head under the covers, knowing exactly where to take this conversation.

Reaching his shaft, she slowly began rolling her tongue over the top of his manhood.

Ceasar's eyes roll back as she begins to fondle his nuts with one hand while jacking him off with the other.

The girl had rhythm.

"Sssshit..." Ceasar moans.

Tory knew circumstantially that she had the upper

hand by disregarding the condoms on the dresser. They would normally use them, but she quickly climbed on top of Ceasar and began her journey with a slow thrusting ride.

He... being in a completely obliviated bliss, never even noticed the slick move.

She then went into overdrive.

Tory had been longing to get this opportunity for the past 18 months... and now, she was actually getting it... *Ceasar's seed.*

Tory put her best cowgirl impersonation into play. She wanted to be in sync with Ceasar. She wanted to feel him... make him feel her, and as soon as he came, she did too, creaming all over him before collapsing into his arms.

Two minutes into trying to catch their breath, Ceasar regained his composure enough to actually speak.

"Damn, bitch... you trying to smother a nigga with all that pussy or what? And get your fat ass up," he added with a slight chuckle.

"Fuck you nigga, you lucky that I even gave your bullshit ass a shot of this pussy. My baby daddy would kill me if he knew that I left the club with yo ass." And Tory was serious.

Ceaser responded with, "Whatever. But *aye,* check this out... I'm about to shower up and get out of here. You know that check out is at 11 o'clock, so after you wash your ass, turn in the key card for me."

"Yeah, aight," she replied, " and damn, you could leave a bitch something to blow on."

"Blow on deez," Ceasar cranks, grabbing himself, but nah, I got you though."

Ceasar checks the time and leaves to take a quick shower.

After getting his swag back in check, he puts his $130k diamond-encrusted chain on and slides out the door.

Now smelling the fresh, crisp scent of one of his newest, most recently purchased cologne, Ceasar pulled out half a blunt of *dro,* compliments of last night, and fired it up.

When he reached his car, he noticed the guts of a cigar stuck to the window of his Benz... this was an S550 model, so it gave him more of a business-like feel when out in the streets.

"Drunk ass bitch, " he mumbled to himself, knowing where they had come from.

Chirp

Ceasar got into his car. He was already pressed for time, so he decided to pick up the pounds from the storage and then drop them off to Deon himself. Knowing that it goes against his teachings of keeping his hands clean, he usually designated his driver to handle pick-ups and drop-offs.

Shortly thereafter

Placing the last package in the trunk, Ceasar then locks the storage space back up and calls Deon.

"Aye yo... D, " Ceasar says after he hears Deon pick up.

"Wazzam, thug?" Deon replies.

"I'm in route," Ceasar added, "... and don't have me waiting outside too long, bro."

"What the fuck? Where is your runner, Amber?"

"Shiidddd, she wasn't answering, so I just said fuck it... I'll take care of the shit myself. Plus, you whining like a little bitch 'bout getting down the road, so shit, you shouldn't even be tripping."

Deon shot a joke toward Ceasar...

"Man... let me find out that you being soft on these hoes, dawg. I thought that you was Mr. Magic Don Juan himself?"

"C'mon fam...," Ceasar tells him, "you know that I keep my foot on a bitch neck at all times. Straight stomp down with it. But yo, I'm getting on I-20 right now."

"Aight... bet that."

Deon disconnects and finishes packing his bag.

Get 'me, Jeezy. I got 'em...

Get 'em, Jeezy. I got 'em...

Ceasar sings along with his go-to CD that he used anytime he was in a dope boy mood.

As he was switching lanes, he felt his cell phone vibrate, indicating that he had a message.

He takes his eyes off the road for a split second and opens the message.

It's from Amber.

Am: Just getting up, baby. Wassup?

Just as Ceasar begins to text her back, something strange happens. He begins to feel thuds in the ground.

"Damn, am I tripping?" He asks himself right before he notices that now he's veering off the road.

Then, in an attempt to check his rearview for any traffic that may have been coming up on him from the rear, he sees a squad car closing in on him with their lights already flashing.

"Damn... you have got to be fuckin' kidding me." "I'm."

He thought about it... and for a brief second, he thought about hitting it and trying to go for it, but knowing how it probably would've ended up, he settled on just pulling over and trying his luck.

Nervous as hell, he did all he could to try to calm himself down while keeping his hands on the steering wheel, awaiting the officer's instructions.

When the cop finally reached Ceasar's door, Ceasar rolled down his window and turned off his loud music.

The Officer Speaks First

"Good Morning. Are you aware that you were drifting off into the emergency line back there?"

Ceasar answers.

"Yes, sir. Just a little tired, I guess. Worked a double shift, and I'm just now getting off from last night's shift," he lied.

The cop asked for the usual... license and registration, and Ceasar obliged, reaching into his glove box to retrieve the items.

"Here you are, sir," he tells the officer while handing over his credentials.

"Thanks," the officer says with an added implication, "Have you been smoking any? This vehicle wreaks of a strong odor of marijuana or something."

"No, sir," Ceasar tells him with a straight face, "I don't even smoke weed, sir. Are you sure that it's coming from this car?"

"Look, Mr. Andrews..." the officer says, turning serious, "We can do this the easy way... or the hard way. It's your choice," he says after giving Ceasar a brief second to weigh out his options.

Ceasar swallowed hard, still trying to keep himself calm, but there were a few beads of sweat that had formed on his forehead, which became a dead giveaway.

The cop then jumped into action... "Please step out of the vehicle for me," he tells Ceasar.

Ceasar does as told, and things go sideways.

"Now turn around and put your hands behind your back."

"What the fuck?!?!" Ceasar spat, "Hell naw... what the fuck am I under arrest for?"

"You're not being arrested... only detained for now," the cop tells him, "Unless there is something in this car that I need to know about."

Ceasar's mind kicked into overdrive.

"Who even gave you the right to search my shit?" He asked the police, then continued on with, "I didn't give you consent, so right now... you're violating my rights."

The officer explains...

"Mr. Andrews... I smelled the scent of marijuana coming out of your car the second you rolled down your window, which now gives me probable cause to search. I'm going to put you in the back of my squad car. So if you would, just have a seat, and if everything checks out, you'll be on your way...sir," the cop tells him.

He puts Ceasar into the police squad car.

Knowing that his trunk was the temporary home to 50lbs of high-grade marijuana that most now call *KUSH*, Ceasar couldn't help but drop his head in defeat. This was it...

"What the fuck did I do to deserve this shit?" He asked himself.

2

———

CENTRAL BOOKING

"Listen for your names to be called. When you hear your name... line up against the wall in a single file line," a large, overweight female detention officer screams.

Twenty minutes into arriving at the downtown jail facility, Ceasar was already beginning to see way too many familiar faces. And this was happening at a time when he really didn't want to be bothered.

He had watched the officer pop the trunk to his Mercedes, and from that moment on, he had seen his freedom slipping away and gotten sick to his stomach.

He snapped back to the present...

"Ceaz!!! Waddup, nigga? What the fuck you doing up in this bitch?"

It was an old customer that Ceasar used to serve long before he had moved up to weight.

Actually, Ceasar was a little excited to see him.

"Robot! Is that you?" Ceasar asked now, smiling a bit.

"In the flesh, Baby Boy. Still making it do what it do," Robot tells him.

Being one who has always been good at observation had taken Ceasar far in the game. He immediately notices the change in Robot.

"Damn, life must be treating you good. I see you finally got your weight back. You gave it up, huh?" He asked.

"Yeah, Youngblood," Robot tells him, "It took a lot of hard days and even harder nights, but God seen me through. Now I'm seven years clean and sober, and I will never smoke crack again."

The thing is... Robot was once a pimp in South Dallas back in the day. It was said that he was also big on snorting cocaine, throwing nice luxurious parties, and buying cars that people in the hood would only be able to see on TV.

He kept a stable of ten of the finest hoes you could imagine, and they all came from different backgrounds. But his weakness was for this blond-haired white girl named Heather.

Heather was his bottom bitch who was in charge of keeping all his hoes on time, on point, and taken care of. She somehow would put you in mind of Marilyn Monroe, but her body stood out from most white chicks.

Her breasts sat up perfectly and firm, which always

allowed her to walk around without a bra... which was most of the time.

As one from back then would tell you, most men fell in love with her hips and her ass, saying that they had never seen a white girl with an ass like that, that poked out so far.

In this day and age, people would probably think that she had ass shots or something.

One day, Robot had walked in on Heather, who had been doing heroin downstairs in a guest bathroom of his 3-story penthouse unbeknownst to him.

Heather, high out of her mind, was in a deep nod when he found her. She was wedged in between the toilet and the bathtub.

Still not knowing that she was on what people nowadays call *boy,* Robot just figured that Heather was tired from being out for three days straight.

He picked her up, carried her back into the bedroom area, and laid her across the bed to rest.

Upon returning to the bathroom, he just so happened to glance at the small pocket mirror of hers that she had left on the countertop. It had lines still left on it, something that she had always done.

He grabbed a seat on the toilet and picked up the mirror.

"Bitch always leaving leftovers," he spat as he pinched off one nostril in order to sniff with the other.

Robot snorted a drug that he thought would be cocaine.

"What the fuck?" He said aloud. But life was hitting

him differently at that moment, and by the time Robot had made it through that first rush, it was too late... there was no turning back.

"Ceasar Andrew's! David Jones! Alex...."

The heavy-set guard was yelling and calling out names for the next arraignment court.

"Aye... look out, Robot," Ceasar said, knowing what the next move was, "they calling us."

"Damn...'bout time. Man, these seats hurt my ass like a mutha. Hey... did you get a chance to use the phone, Youngblood?" Robot asked as an afterthought.

"Nah, O.G... I'm just gonna wait until after court so I'll *know* what's going on."

Ceasar and Robot, along with a few other cats, made their way through the crowded area of Central Booking into the courtroom.

The chairs were separated for women to be seated on one side and the men to be seated on the other.

A terrible smell began to form as the guards piled every bit of 60 people into this one room.

Now, sitting here waiting for the Judge to come out, Ceasar couldn't help but think about him violating his probation. The last time he stepped in a courtroom like this, the result was a Judge sentencing him to 10 years probation. So, now... being *back* in the same situation, he knew that the worst was yet to come.

In came the Judge.

"When I call your name, please stand," the Judge stated, "I will inform you of your charge or charges, your bond, and ask you if you have a lawyer. Please hold all questions until the very end."

Ceasar could already see Robot's knee bouncing. A clear indication of Robot's nervousness.

"Ceasar Andrews," the Judge calls, "You are being held on Possession of Marijuana with a bond of $50,000 cash or surety... and a Probation Violation, no bond.

She continued... "Do you have an attorney, or will you be needing for the State to appoint you one?"

"I have one, Ma'am," Ceasar told her.

The Judge was a female.

"Ok, you may be seated," she told him.

Ceasar flopped into his seat with his head slumped.

He was at a loss for words.

All he could do now was sit and think about all the ways he could have avoided this situation. Somehow, the day had already gone from him feeling like he was on top of the world to him now feeling like he was at the bottom of the barrel.

Time seemed to stop as the Judge continued to call out names and charges.

Twenty minutes had passed, and the Judge had started to wrap things up when she exited the courtroom; that guard who had led them in magically reappeared.

Ceasar was just coming to terms with the situation that he was now faced with as he noticed that the room was being emptied out. But he noticed that he was one of the last ones to leave the room. Instead of being led back into the waiting area with the TVs, this time, they were sent to a large cell with 15 payphones that were spread out evenly along the walls around the entire place.

There were a few smaller cells with bars that were used to detain those who didn't follow orders too well.

Ceasar knew now what he was facing and what the situation called for. It was time to make a few phone calls and to get his lawyer on the line *and* on the ball.

Ring

Ring

Ring

Ring

"Hello... Frank's Office of Law. How may I help you?" He heard a voice say.

"Hey, Jessica, this is Mr. Andrews," he said matter of factly, "*please* tell me that Frank is in the office right now."

Jessica recognized his name and his voice.

"Oh, hey, Ceasar. I'm sorry, but he's down at the courthouse already this morning. Is there a message or something that you'd like for me to pass on?"

"Yeah... please," Ceasar answered, "Tell him that I'm being held down here at the Lew Sterrett Jail and that I need him to come visit me before the day ends."

Even in the wake of hearing the news of Ceasar's situation, Jessica never broke stride with her job's responsibility or her role of professionalism.

She answered, and across the jail's monitored phone line, Ceasar heard...

"Okay, no problem. I'm sure that he won't mind making that happen for you, Mr. Andrews. Anything else?"

"Nah, that's it. Thank you."

Before hanging up, he heard…

"Alright. Bye."

Having his lawyer come to visit him would help him sleep better at night.

But it was now time for him to start thinking a few more steps ahead of the game just in case the future didn't pan out like he would like.

Before making his next call, Ceasar sat and gave himself a second to clear his mind and time to collect his thoughts. He was surrounded by 30 other guys, all trying to accomplish the same thing that he was trying to accomplish. To get out.

Living this *Dope Boy* lifestyle, he also knew that there would always be a possibility that he could get locked up at any time. But…he never expected that it would happen so soon.

****

Ceasar was only 20 years old, and he already owned two barbershops, a janitorial service, and supplied more than half of the dealers in Dallas with their drugs.

He got his first break in the year 2000 at the early age of 14 when he used to help his crippled uncle get around town and run his routes.

His time back then consisted of going to school all

day long and, after that, rushing home to assist his Uncle Charles with *his* hustle and routine. They would be out all the rest of the evening, sometimes up until 2 or 3 in the morning, doing what seemed to be just going from house to house.

Ceasar never fully understood why his Uncle would always carry a briefcase in and out of those houses back then because, as far as he understood, it only seemed normal to see briefcases in the hands of men who wore suits and worked in or out of offices. It was weird.

Uncle Charles always had money. He had luxury cars; these were the cars that he would have Ceasar driving him around in.

One day, Charles seemed a little uneasy, and Ceasar had taken notice that he had been arguing on the phone for a while with some Mexican dude. Funny…but he was even arguing in Spanish with the dude.

This led to the situation at the next house that they were due to arrive at. The Mexicaan's house. But instead of waiting in the car as he usually did, Uncle Charles had made Ceasar come in this time.

It was an old, run-down, and low-class house in the middle of the slums.

But when you stepped inside, there were hardwood floors, expensive furnishings, TVs, and surveillance camera monitors everywhere. They were showing what was happening everywhere outside of the house.

A huge Mexican guy with a star tattooed on the side of his head had answered the door. He appeared to have stood over 6 feet and probably weighed well over 300 pounds.

He answered the door carrying a .40 caliber pistol.

As they entered, the big guy said something in Spanish and directed them to have a seat while he disappeared somewhere behind them. Then, after he had gotten out of earshot range, Ceasar's uncle leaned over to him and whispered, "No matter what happens here today… keep your mouth shut. You hear me?"

He added, "Real niggas never tell shit," and with that, the big Mexican came back into the living room, speaking Spanish to the older of the two… Charles.

Charles followed him to the back.

Before reaching the hallway, he stopped at the turn of the corner and said, "Stay put, and remember… don't say shit".

Ceasar could sense that something was wrong, but he decided that he would wait until he and his uncle were back in the car before he asked.

Ten minutes went by.

Twenty more minutes went by, and then Ceasar began to worry.

After a few more minutes of worrying, he finally heard something that sounded like arguing again.

The young 14-year-old boy crept as quietly as he possibly could toward the corner. After peeking around it into the doorway of the backroom, he paused. Ceasar couldn't believe his eyes.

His uncle, the oversized Mexican, and some gray-haired mob-looking guy in a suit all had one another standing and froze at gunpoint... It mattered then; everything switched, and all of a sudden, everything started moving in slow motion.

Everything...

Guns were going off, and bullets were flying through the air in every direction. Ceasar even pissed on himself from being so scared.

Seconds later, after the coast seemed clear and there was no more movement, Ceasar ran into the room. No one was moving or even seemed alive, for all that matters.

He fell and collapsed at his uncle's side.

Now crying with his head down, he heard the sound of Charles trying to say something.

"Listen, Lil Man," his uncle grunted out, "I'm not gonna make it. You see all this stuff on that table over there?"

Ceasar looked up and saw what looked like a bunch of white square packages and a lot of big bags of grass.

His uncle continued…

"Take it all and bag it all up and then put that shit in the trunk and go home."

Ceasar looked at him with a slightly confused look on his face.

"Put it all in the attic, and when the time comes, you'll know what to do with it."

"But what about you, Uncle Charles?" He asked, "I can't leave you like this. I need you," Caesar said through streams of tears.

"Don't worry about me...this old boy done had his

run. Just remember to do what your Uncle Charles told you. And look...real niggas never tell shit. You hear me?"

That was Charles' last breath... and words.

****

"Youngblood...youngblood," Robot was saying repeatedly, waking Ceasar from out of his sleep, "Aye, the phone is on you now."

Ceasar stood up and began slowly walking over to the phone.

He knew who he had to call...

"Rico..." he said, whispering to himself.

3

RICO

The day was still young when Rico pulled up to one of the local drug houses over on the south side of Oak Cliff.

Ring

Ring

"What's up?"

It was J.J. who answered. He was one of Rico's top Lieutenants and the one in charge of all the houses on the south end of Interstate 35.

Rico snapped… "What up, nigga? You know I'm out front. Send Chase to open the gate!"

He ended the call without even waiting for a response.

A couple of minutes had passed, and as if Rico wasn't already irritated, he was fuming now that the young boy, Chase, was taking so long to get outside.

Pulling around to the back of the house, he exited the car carrying a Louis Vuitton backpack.

It was 90 degrees outside. He had chosen to make it a casual day by wearing an all-white YSL short set with gray GUCCI loafers… soft bottoms. Seeing that it was hot, instead of wearing all of his jewelry, as he usually did, he went with the light and cool approach and wore just a Franco chain and a set of diamond studded earrings that added just the right touch.

But still… he was pissed.

"Next time I pull up, yo ass better be watching those cameras. You think that I wanna be parked outside of a fuckin' trap house waiting on you, little ass nigga?"

"My bad, Big Dawg. It won't happen again," Chase said, trying not to piss Rico off any further than he was.

"Yeah. I know it won't… cause after today yo lil ass is done."

"Come on, Rico," Chase started to plead, "it ain't my…" *SMACK!!!*

Rico silenced the kid with a backhanded slap that sent him sliding in the opposite direction of him and crumbling to the ground.

"Did I ask you for an excuse, homie? Nigga, I pay you to pay attention… not make excuses."

Tired of the back and forth, Rico then headed for the back door, leaving the young Chase behind, still holding his face.

Now, walking into the house, he could tell that business was booming as usual. There were three beautiful naked women all hired to cook his cocaine and turn it into crack once the package came in.

J.J. was sitting at a table counting money that had been made off of last week's package.

Hundred-dollar stacks lay neatly across that same table as he sent the cash through the money counter and wrapped them with rubber bands.

This was no ordinary trap house; it was mainly a spot where they did most of the cooking and distributing.

Instead of taking the risk of doing a lot of drop-offs, Rico made all of his street generals pick up from the closest supply house to them or their spots' locations.

"Rico, my main man," J.J. said, greeting him with a fist pound, "tell me sumn' good in the hood."

Rico reciprocated the verbal gesture with his own...

"What's the word, bird? Tell me sumn' I ain't heard."

And this is how they kicked it.

Rico added, "How's business coming?"

"Shiiddddd... jumpin' like Jordan on this end. We just finished up that last shit, but all the paperwork is on point."

Rico was happy.

"Dats what I'm talking about, young nigga."

Rico stood about 6'3 and weighed 270lbs, which made him a very intimidating guy.

At the age of 18, he was incarcerated for taking part in a credit card scam where he did four years on a seven-year sentence.

While he was locked up, he spent countless days

working out both mentally and physically and plotting for his return. No one came to visit him during that 4-year bid, but he would still occasionally get a letter and money on his books from his childhood friend, Ceasar.

Once he was released, Ceasar was the only one waiting to help him out and to put him back on his feet. Surprisingly, though, when Rico went up the road to prison, Ceasar was 14 years old, still in school, and running his uncle around town to take care of his errands. Upon his return, that's when he found out that his once young, naive shadow had made a name for himself, and seeing that Rico was the older of the two, he stepped into a leading role naturally. And that was when he had noticed that Ceasar had been sitting on a whole lot of weight but seemed to not know the first thing of what to do with it.

Rico's name always rang bells even before he left, but after being released, he attracted even more people.

He had taken Ceasar from making only ten to twenty grand profit every two weeks or so to making $80,000.00 a month.

Things were finally looking up for the duo.

"Damn, nigga. You just gonna hold the blunt, or you gone let me smoke with you?" J.J. asked and then yelled, "Rico!... Rico!" Trying to get his attention.

"Here, nigga... shit. And stop doing all that hollering in my ear. Da fuck wrong with you?" Rico shot at him before screaming across the room, "... aye yo, Keisha!!! Roll me up a blunt of that Girl Scout shit. And you better not put no holes in my shit."

Keisha replied with a bit of a touch of sarcasm…

"Aight, Boss."

Rico's phone rang…

"Hello," he answered.

You have a collect call from Ceasar.

Press 1 to accept the…

Rico quickly pressed 1, accepting Ceasar's phone call from jail.

"What up, Fam…?" Ceasar shot out first.

"Shit, I should be asking you the same thing. Nigga, what the fuck you doing calling me from jail?"

"Man, some ol' fluke ass shit went down this morning. You know that we can't talk how we want to on these phones, so I need you to come visit me so we can run down through there on this shit."

"Already, I got you. Have you already called Frank to put him up on game and tell him what's happening?"

Ceasar answered him…

"Yea… he should be pullin' up on me today or tomorrow sometime."

Rico thought and then spoke…

"Ok. Bet. Look, I'll be down through there probably tomorrow to make sure you're good. But keep your head up, lil bruh."

"Aight then. Bet," Ceasar told him and then disconnected.

The call had taken Rico by surprise because he and Ceasar had been together that night before at *Club Onyx*. The club was more packed than normal, with strippers popping and twerking, doing their best to impress the ballers that turned out.

When he and Ceasar had made it upstairs to their section, they had noticed that across from them and their section, Lil Boosie and his entourage were in attendance enjoying themselves with three of the most popular dancers... Lucious, Gucci, and CinnaBunz.

One-dollar bills covered the floor to the point that you could barely see the carpet. This made Rico feel some type of way because he and Ceasar were usually the ones to attract all of the attention.

He quickly ordered a case of *Ace of Spades* and twenty grand in all one-dollar bills in order to try and steal the show.

Ceasar wasn't as worried about the situation. In fact, he knew Boosie and had previously had conversations with him inquiring about a show that he was trying to put together.

Rico and three more of their crew members started the show by making it rain. As they did that, Ceasar went over to have a few words with the rapper.

Upon returning, he took notice that Tory was making her way over to their section in one of those white string stripper suits with some knee-high black Pradas. She was one of the main faces of *Onyx*, which made her popular amongst most of the girls.

Tory was of a light-skinned complexion... 5'5, hazel eyes with a slim waist that slid down to her apple bottom ass.

Back in the day, they used to call her "NuNu,"

referring to the character played by Lauren London in the hit movie *ATL*, which also starred the Atlanta-born celebrity rapper TI.

That night had turned out to be one to remember… especially after Tory had their section filled with dancers.

When it came time for the club to close, Ceasar and each of his boys had made plans to take a few of the girls home. He and his crew were all waiting in Valet for them to finish getting dressed and exit the building.

Ceasar was in his white S550 Benz, Rico was driving a blue Audi, and their entourage had come in an all-black Tahoe. When the dancers came out, they all filed out into the parking lot in a single line and then went their separate ways.

"Here go your blunt, Daddy… I mean Boss," Rico heard as Keisha purred softly into his ear, causing his manhood to jump in his shorts.

After handing him the lit swisher, she stood behind him in the *La-Z-Boy* recliner that he sat in and began massaging his shoulders.

Keisha was a tall, slender red bone with freckles and sandy red hair.

The guys kept her working at the trap more because of the shape of her ass rather than her cooking skills.

See, the girls weren't allowed to wear clothes while processing the dope, just in case it even ran across their minds to steal. This was a plus for her because knowing how her body was it was a good way to keep her in good graces of the team.

Rico ordered her, "Aye… go put on yo shit. I need to take you by Easy's shop to pick up some supplies."

He went on, "J.J., load that bread into my bag and give the work to the girls to get started. It's Fridayshut, and we need to have shit ready for this week."

"I gotcha, Fam," J.J. answered before Rico continued on…

"I'm taking Keisha's big booty ass with me. I need to get her ready for Ceasar's visit tomorrow."

"Oh yeah… what's up with bro? He good?" J.J. paused for a second to ask.

"I don't know yet," Rico answered, "But that can't slow business down. One man, don't stop *this* show. The show must go on."

"Straight up," said J.J., "But I'm gonna hit you up when we shut down. Bet?"

"Bet," Rico answered.

As Rico pulled off the street, he checked the time and cut the music up on the stereo of his Range Rover. Keisha was in the passenger seat playing with the bubble gum that was in her mouth, twirling it around her finger and then slurping it back up into her mouth.

That was something like a signal to Rico, letting him know that she was in one of her freaky moods.

She unbuckled his seatbelt.

As soon as she did, he was already adjusting his seat and began fumbling with the buckle on the belt of the shorts that he was wearing.

"Just chill, Daddy," she told him, "Let me do all the work. You drive."

With her leaning over the armrest Keisha slipped his dick through the slit of his *POLO RALPH LAUREN* boxers and took his already hardened manhood into her mouth. She two-handed him as she sucked the tip in a fast up-and-down motion.

Keisha knew exactly what to do to make him cum fast. But two minutes into it, Rico had to pull over into one of the *Super 8* motels just to let her finish due to not being able to keep his eyes on the road as she began to get deeper into it.

He would be damned if he risked wrecking his truck.

Keisha began getting a little sloppy and started letting the wetness from her spit drip down his shaft and on down to his balls. She then used her free hand to jack him off all at the same time.

Without warning nor hesitation, out of nowhere, Rico hurriedly grabbed and pulled down the tights that Keisha had on and slid two fingers into her already warm and moist pussy lips.

"Mmmm shit, Daddy. I want this dick," she moaned in between a slurp.

The faster Rico slid his fingers in and out of her pulsating juice spot, the harder she sucked. Just as he was about to bust deep into the back of her throat, his cell phone rang.

RING!

"Fuck!" He shouted.

"Hey, Bruh-Bruh… what you got going?" Diamond asked as soon as he had answered.

"Oh, what's up, Lil One?" Rico countered, almost out of breath, "shit, just out and about doing a little running around. Wazzam?"

"Man, I've been blowing Ceasar's line up all day," Diamond told him, "Have you talked to him?" She asked.

"Yeah, I have. As a matter of fact, I need to meet up with you 'bout that. Where you at?"

"I'm at *Rudy's* grabbing me a three-piece chicken. Why don't you meet me at *Race Trak* on Ledbetter in about 30 minutes?"

Rico agreed and was ready to get off the phone in order to finish what Keisha had started before Diamon interrupted them.

"One," Diamond had said when she had ended the call.

But after quick thought, Rico grabbed the back of Keisha's hair, pulling her by her braids to get her off his dick.

"Damn, Daddy, you're gonna pull a bitch hair out," she cried.

"Look," Rico began telling her while handing her a wad of cash, "Take this and go check in a room. Text me the room number soon as you get settled, and I'll be back later tonight".

He then grabbed a small ziplock bag out of his pocket containing some dro and a few ecstasy pills.

Keisha began straightening her clothes.

"Hurry back," she told him, "You know Imma be waitin on that dick."

"Girl, get yo ass up outta here. I got somewhere to be in a minute."

On the way to the meet-up spot that he and Diamond had agreed to, Rico was trying to figure out a way to break the news to her that Ceasar was locked up.

"Damn," he said to himself, "This is fucked up."

4

REALITY HITS

Rico pulled into an empty parking spot at the gas station a few minutes early to make sure that it was a good place to meet.

He didn't want to be sitting somewhere that the police would be patrolling, seeing that he had $ 70,000 in his bag sitting on the passenger side floor.

Figuring that he probably had enough time, Rico ran inside the store to grab a few cigarillos for the *Kush* that he had in his glove box. As soon as he was finishing up rolling the first blunt, he noticed Diamond pulling up in her pink BMW 330i.

He flashed his lights, letting her know to pull up and park next to him.

Diamond quickly hopped into the truck with him.

"Damn nigga, that's some gas gas," she said as soon as she had sat down in the passenger seat, "What you rolling up?"

"The last of dem cookies we had," Rico told her, "We gone need to reload on the *Dro* asap, Lil Sis."

The conversation proceeded without Diamond even having a clue yet. Her next statement forced Rico to hit her with the news without beating around the bush.

"Why don't you tell Ceasar," she said matter of factly, "I got to go pick up the bricks from Hector, so *he* needs to be the one to handle that."

With his eyes staring straight forward, Rico didn't want to look Diamond in the eye when he told her. But he had to tell her.

"Lil Sis… ummm, Diamond. I don't know how to say this, but I *have* to say it. Ceaz is locked up."

Dead silence hit the cabin of Rico's truck interior.

He continued...

"I found out earlier today when he called me from Lew Sterrett…"

"Locked up?" She asked, interrupting him, "... are you fucking kiddin me?... for what?"

She dropped her head in frustration…

"He hasn't even called me to let me know that he's OK. What happened? Have you talked to Frank yet?"

Diamond shot question after question until Rico stopped her mid-sentence.

"Dee, calm down and just breathe for a second."

As he began to try and console her, he lit the Kush blunt, took a few hits himself, and then passed it to her.

Diamond puffed on it a few times, inhaled in as much smoke as she possibly could, and then exhaled.

Rico gave her a minute before speaking...

"Now check this out." He began slowly, "Everything will be OK. We just gotta stay strong and continue to handle business. You know that Ceasar would have called you by now. But what's rule number one?... one head don't contact the other head from the inside, right?"

"You right, Bruh Bruh. I'm just trippin out because he's on probation, and Ceaz is supposed to be under the radar right now."

Rico understood.

"I feel you. I'm going to visit him tomorrow night so we can figure out what's really going on. Wednesday's gonna be his next visitation day, and I'm sure that he'll be expecting to see you by then. So, wipe them tears and get yourself together. You know, Bro, don't want you out here shedding tears and shit."

Diamond quickly wiped her face and passed the blunt back to him. After that, she then took a second to gather herself and to refocus.

"You good?" Rico asked.

"Yeah, I'm straight," Diamond said, still with a bit of disappointment in her voice.

Rico jumped back on course.

"Now, back on the business. I got the rest of that paper for the last shipment right there under your foot. It's 70 bands in all," he told her.

"OK, cool. I'm gonna reload, and we should be good by Wednesday morning. You got enough to last you until then?"

Rico thought about the trap.

"Yeah… it's getting whipped up right now. Just hit me and let me know when it's game time. Imma let you know what Ceaz is hollering bout."

"Aight. Thank you, Rico. If you wasn't here, I don't know what I would have done. Hit me up when you know sumn," she said, leaning over to give him the brotherly hug like she usually did.

Right before she got out, he noticed another female in the car with Diamond.

"Who dat is, Lil Sis?"

"Oh, that's ya girl, Angie. You know she been tryna fuck wit you for a minute. She *just* said sumn about fucking with you tonite… and you know that the little bitch bout that life."

Rico saw the opportunity rising before him.

"Shiiddddd… tell her to come ride wit a real nigga for the night," he replied, rubbing his hand over the deep-cut waves in his hair.

"Bet… you know I got you, Bro," Diamond told him, "Just make sure she gets up early tomorrow. We gotta shoot out by 7."

"Wouldn't have it any other way."

Diamond hopped out of the truck, throwing the brown *Gucci* bag into her backseat, and slid back into the driver's side.

After a minute of talking, Angie grabbed her Birkin bag and ran over to jump in the Range with Rico. He had already started the engine and was ready to pull off.

Pulling out of the gas station, he inserted Lil

Webbie's Savage *Life* album. He put on a song to set the mood.

> *"Mane look...you my gutta bitch*
> *who I'm wit when I'm in shit*
> *wit my other bitch."*

The two 12" speakers gave the song a real nice edge, causing his rearview mirror to shake uncontrollably.

"Ouhhhhhh, that's my jam!!!" Angie screamed, lifting her arms to the sky and bobbing her head to the beat.

Stopping at a red light, Rico took a second to get a good look at her grooving to the song. She had the body of one of those runway models… slim and petite, but her ass was thick and perfect in shape.

The mole on her face complemented her brown skin, giving her this school girl look.

He thought to himself… "This is going to be a night to remember."

Rico was planning on taking Angie back to the room where Keisha was and having a wild ass threesome.

First, he'd stop by the local liquor store to get two boxes of magnums, a bottle of *Patron*, and some more *Swisher Sweet* cigars. After that, the rest would fall into place.

*****

On the way to the room, Rico passed the cigars to Angie and instructed her to roll them all.

"Damn, Baby… who gone be smoking all this damn weed? You got three cups. Where the third head at?" She asked.

"Why do you ask so many questions?" Rico asked with a sly and furtive grin.

But still answering her, he told her, "If you must know, Lil Keisha at the room waiting on us. We gone have us a private party tonight. Just the three of us," he added.

"Umph, umph, umph," the girl answered, "Boy, you nasty."

"Naw, but we *bout* to get nasty," he replied, sliding his fingers between her legs and massaging her clit.

"Boy, you better stop before we not even make it to the room," Angie told him, still spreading her thighs a bit wider.

At a second thought, she asked, "Oh yeah, you talkin' 'bout big booty Keisha from Glendale?"

Rico was surprised.

"Yeah, how you know KeKe?"

"That's my bitch. We went to grade school together. Watch… you gone see."

The rest of the ride was spent with Rico on the phone, giving orders and directing traffic. After pulling into the hotel, they both exited the truck and headed up the stairs to the room that Keisha had sent him the address for and checked into.

Knock

Knock

Keisha answered the door wearing nothing but a bath towel, then turned around and quickly walked back over to the mirror.

Stopping in her tracks, she noticed a familiar reflection in the mirror.

"Bitchhh! Oh my God, where the fuck you been!" Keisha screamed.

"Shit, where ain't I been?" Angie replied, "It's been a minute since I seen yo ass."

"Speaking of ass. Damn bitch, look at all that ass in that skirt. You betta work."

Angie turned around, bouncing her ass and making one ass cheek jump at a time.

Rico was just now getting off the phone as he was sitting down on the bed.

Sitting the bottle of *Patron* on one of the nightstands, he pulled out a blunt of Dro and lit it.

"Where them pills at KeKe?" Rico asked.

"Here you go, Daddy."

Keisha handed him the ziplock bag and started to walk back over to Angie until he grabbed her by the waist.

"Hold up, hold up…not so fast. Angie, come here right quick," he commanded, pulling some X pills out of the bag, "… I want both of y'all to climb on to the bed on all fours…doggy style."

"Daddy, can we at least get a little drank in us first before we start this show?" Asked one of the girls.

"What I say?"

Doing as told, they both climbed onto the bed side by side. Rico removed the towel from Keisha and lifted the skirt that Angie was wearing.

Using both hands at the same time and almost simultaneously, he began to play with both of their pussies, finding each of their pearl tongues.

As they became more and more wet, he started to transfer the juices from their clits to their anus. Once wet enough, he then took an X pill in each hand and inserted them into the anus of each Keisha and Angie.

"Oooh shit, Daddy," they screamed in unison.

Rolling over to their backs, they began to play with themselves as Rico went to the nightstand to put the blunt out and grab the bottle of liquor.

Uncorking the bottle, he took a massive gulp and passed it around. Three rotations. He then sat in a chair facing the bed and watched the freak show unravel.

First, the girls started tongue-kissing one another. Keisha helped Angie peel off the few layers of clothes that she still had on.

After pushing Keisha onto her back, Angie flipped upside down, straddling her in the 69 position.

After a few minutes of watching Rico then got up and completely removed his clothes until all he had left on was socks. He then moved himself closer to the *situation*. Angie took him into her mouth as he positioned himself over her while lifting and spreading Keisha's legs over his shoulders and emerging his face into her pussy juices.

The formation looked like a triangle with Rico

eating Keisha, Keisha eating Angie, and Angie giving him head.

Within a couple of seconds, the mood went from crazy to intense.

Rico switched up and began pounding Angie from the back while she was face down and screaming into Keisha.

With each thrust, he created a wave on her ass, forcing her further and further into Keisha's pussy.

Next, he laid them on top of each other, going from one to the other, sliding in and out at an even faster speed. At one point, the rhythm had become so pleasurable. Keisha, who was on top, came so hard that she squirted… causing her to cream all over Angie's pulsating clit.

Seconds later, Angie, too, had climaxed, collapsing onto the bed. Rico then laid back on the bed, legs spread, inviting them to come to finish the job.

Angie sucked the tip and shaft of his dick, and Keisha concentrated on the balls.

Two minutes in, he grabbed both of their heads, directing them to the tip so they could both taste him.

Rico began to squirt into their faces.

All in one movement, they licked him clean until they all collapsed and exhausted onto the bed.

The night had gone by so fast for the trio.

Before finally falling asleep, they fucked again and even showered together.

The sun was coming up.

The clock read 6 o'clock am.

Ring

Ring

"Aye," Rico answered.

"Damn, Big Bro… sounds like a long night just ended," Diamond joked.

"Dead ass," Rico answered with a slight chuckle.

"Shoot me the address and tell my girl to get up, wash her ass and be ready. We gotta get on the road."

"Bet," he answered.

Rico ended the call by texting her directions to the hotel.

The room was dimly lit, but he could see the girls curled up on each side of him and still sleeping.

Sliding out of the bed, he opened the blinds to let the sunlight brighten the room, causing both Keisha and Angie to wake up instantly.

After sparking one of the unfinished blunts from the night before, Rico turned on the shower and instructed them to freshen up and get ready so they could move around.

Thirty minutes later, Diamond was pulling into the *Super 8*, texting…

I'm outside…

They all left the room together, leaving *Housekeeping* with one hell of a mess to clean up.

The girls said their goodbyes while Diamond and Rico made plans to set up a meeting for when she returned.

After Angie hopped in the car with Diamond, Rico

gave them both a thumbs up and sent them about their way.

Everyone seemed happy for the moment, and they all knew the assignment.

All was well… considering.

5

CEASAR

The day had gone by quite slowly after the visit with Frank, Ceasar's lawyer. He had expected Frank to be able to handle this situation with no problems, but it was starting to look like this was going to be harder than he thought.

After being put on probation from his last case two years ago, the judge made it clear that he didn't want to see his face again. Judge Brown had placed him on a ten-year felony probation.

Frank's goal was to either get him reinstated on his probation or get the minimum amount of jail time possible.

Returning to his cell after seeing his lawyer, Ceasar could do nothing but think about Diamond and the situation that he had left her in. Together, they built a well-organized drug distribution network in eight different cities within Texas, Louisiana, Arkansas, and Oklahoma.

Over the years, he had taught Diamond all she needed to know about controlling the market and operating their team with an iron fist.

At the age of sixteen, Ceasar had made a name for himself for being a young overnight success in the dope game. While most guys his age were going to school trying to earn a scholarship with good grades or playing ball, he was actually *balling* and *trying* to keep interest in school.

His mother had died while he was only three years old due to an overdose of heroin, which forced him to move in with his uncle. After his uncle's death, he was left to fend for himself.

The house and car were left in his possession, forcing him to step up and take responsibility for things he had no experience of handling. During the first couple of months, Ceasar continued with his regular schedule of going to school, going home, and being a normal kid.

His distant aunt tried countless times to get him to move out to California with her and his two cousins, but he always refused.

After only three months, the bills were beginning to fall behind, and the car was in need of a serious tune-up.

One day, after a long, stressful day at school, Ceasar decided to try to unwind by kicking it with one of his close friends, Melvin, that evening.

"Man… I'm starving, fam. You ain't got nothing in the ice box at the crib?" Asked Melvin.

"Hell nah, you know it's been really tough for me lately. It was my 15th birthday last week, and I spent it sitting in the house watching music videos," Ceasar told him.

"Damn, bro. Why didn't you tell me? You know that me and Chelsey could have rescheduled our plans, and I would have fucked witcha," Melvin said, speaking of his girlfriend.

"I wasn't trippin," Ceasar told him, sounding more depressed, "I really wasn't feeling it anyway."

Melvin was hearing nothing of it.

"Fuck dat, we doing sumn today. It's all on me. I'ma hit Chelsey and tell her to get with her cousin Diamond and we hitting da town."

Caesar tried fighting against it.

"Man, you know it's a school night. They might not even be able to get out of the house."

"I got this, Ceasar. Dang… you just go home and jump fresh. I'll call you soon as it's game time."

And that was it.

When Ceasar did arrive home, his mood went from depressed to disaster when he discovered that the lights were off.

In his mind, all he could think of was, "Why me?"

It seemed that if it wasn't one thing, it was another.

After taking a quick wash-off, he texted Melvin to let him know that he would be ready in ten minutes.

Using the light from his cell phone, Ceasar picked

out a pair of black *Levi* jeans, a plain white V-neck tee shirt, and a pair of black, red, and white *Air Jordans* to match.

Ring

Ring

"Yeah," Ceasar answered.

"Come on nigga, we outside," he heard from the other side of the line.

"Here I come," Ceasar replied, hanging up while heading out the door.

The ride to *Hooters* was pretty quiet.

Ceasar never really said too much after introducing himself to the girls. Upon arriving downtown at the restaurant, they chose to sit in a booth close to the window nearest to the bar area.

The place was actually pretty packed for a Thursday night, and a lot of the restaurantgoers had worn their football jerseys and were watching the big screen TV monitors that were spread all around the room.

Melvin was a little older, so he was the one who had done most of the talking when it came time to order.

"Welcome to *Hooters*. May I take your order?" The waitress asked.

She was a beautiful blonde chick with large, perfect-sized breasts.

She wore bright red lipstick with orange *short* shorts.

The cut-off T-shirt that she wore read *Hooters*.

"Yea, can I get an order of fifty boneless hot wings, two sides of fries, and a jumbo *Bahama Mama*… please?"

That was alcohol.

"Of course, sir. Can I see some ID?"

"Yes, Ma'am," Melvin quickly answered and obliged her.

Melvin and Chelsey were always going out, so they made it mandatory to keep an ID that said, they were twenty-one when they actually were seventeen.

The ID did it, and as the waitress was handing it back to Melvin, she stated, "Thank you. I'll have that right out."

As the night wore on, the air between the group became a little less thicker. Melvin and Chelsey slid off to the balcony, and Ceasar continued to sit with Diamond near the window that looked out into the busy downtown Dallas streets.

"So, how old are you, Mr. Caesar?" Diamond had asked

"Just turned fifteen last week," he told her.

"Ohhh. I hate I missed the big day," Diamond said to him, sounding sincere, "I know your family did it big, huh?"

"Actually, I don't have any family. My mama died when I was only 3. I was living with my uncle, but he just died a few months back, too. So now I stay by myself?"

The conversation continued another 15 minutes until Diamond froze in her place with her mouth wide open. When Ceasar turned to see what she was looking at, he saw an older woman walking in their direction. His eyes had to be playing tricks on him, or the liquor had really taken a hold on him. The woman looked *exactly* like Diamond, only grown and more developed.

"Oh," the woman said, going straight in on Diamond, "So you lie to me and say that you and Chelsey were studying at her house… just to sneak out to be with some nappy head ass lil *boy*?"

She then slapped Diamond in the face.

"You little hot-tailed bitch! When you get home, I want all of your shit packed up and out of my house before I get there. Do I make myself understood?"

It took a second for Diamond to actually answer, but she did.

"Yes, Ma'am," she finally forced herself to say as she cried and held her face.

As the women stormed off, Diamond balled herself up in the corner of the booth and cried her eyes out.

Sensing that it was time to go, Ceasar requested the check, found Melvin, and gave them the rundown of what had just happened.

Melvin paid the tab, and the group headed for the car. It was time to call it a night. On the way home, Ceasar rode in the back, holding Diamond while attempting to console her.

Before exiting the car, he told her to call him if she ever needed anything and gave her his cell phone number. He then walked into the house, returning to his own dilemma.

The lights were still out.

After finding an emergency backup light, he placed

it in his room and began staring at the ceiling until he lost himself in his thoughts and dozed off.

Ring

Ring

"Hello," Ceasar answered without paying attention to the caller ID.

"Ceasar, I need you," he heard Diamond saying, "She did it. My mama really beat me up and threw me out."

"What!!!" He exclaimed, sitting straight up in his bed, "Where are you?"

"At the Leadbetter station," Diamond replied, voice cracking, "I'm scared... please come get me."

"Aight... I'm on my way."

After getting off the phone, Ceasar snapped and realized that he had said that he was on his way.

But how?

It had been months since he had driven his uncle's Mercedes because it had been on camera when he had driven it away from the house of the Mexicans at the time when his uncle was killed.

But tonight, he was going to take his chances because he felt like Diamond really needed him.

After letting the car warm up for a minute, he reversed out of the driveway and headed to pick her up.

The drive wasn't far, but it seemed like forever getting to her due to his mind racing and all the crazy thoughts that were dancing in and out of his mind.

Finally, he made it to her.

By the time they arrived back at Ceasar's house, she was sound asleep.

He had to carry her in.

Once inside, he laid her across his bed, closed the bedroom door, and went to lie down on the couch.

The night faded into total darkness.

When he finally awakened, he realized that the sun had come up. He wiped the crust from his eyes and instantly noticed a familiar smell of something that he hadn't smelled in a long time.

Breakfast.

Walking through the house towards the Kitchen, he noticed that the lights were back on, and that *music* was playing loudly through the house.

Entering the kitchen, he saw Diamond wearing one of his t-shirts with her hair wrapped in a towel, indicating that she had just gotten out of the shower.

She was 17, but her body had already filled out in so many places.

Her high yellow skin and long, silky hair made her stand out amongst most girls her age.

"Damn… breakfast?" Ceasar said, more like asking as he walked in, almost scaring her to death.

"Boy, don't be sneaking up on me like that. Haven't you ever heard of the relationship between a black woman and a frying pan?"

"Oh yeah? Well, I guess I'm the lucky one."

"Here," Diamond said, handing him a plate of food, "You really are. Have a seat. I know you're starving. It looks like you ain't ate in days."

Ceasar had a seat at the dining room table as she fixed herself a plate.

"So, how did you manage to get these lights back on?"

"Well, we got this dude over in our hood named Run Run... he's a smoker. He's known for cutting on people's lights and fixing it to where the electric company never knows."

"Oh, OK... how much do he be charging? You should have woke me up; I would have took care of it."

"No offense," Diamond told him, "But if it was like that, you would have paid the bill on time. Plus, I owed you one for coming through for me last night."

She then grabbed a seat directly across from him.

"Thanks," he told her.

"So, what you gone do, Ceasar? How you gone continue to keep this house up, pay the bills... not to mention that nice ass car out front?"

"I don't know. Crazy to say," he admitted, "I haven't really thought about it."

Then it hit him.

The attic.

"Can I trust you, D... I mean, Diamond? Like, *really, really* trust you?" He asked, looking with a deeper intent within his eyes.

"Ceasar, after last night, I could never turn on you. You didn't have to come get me, but you did. For that, I will always keep it one hundred with you."

The look in Diamond's eyes told Ceasar that she was serious.

He got up... "Follow me," he told her.

Ceasar then walked from the dining room through

the house to the hallway. Stretching out his arm upward, he then pulled a string that hung from the ceiling to the entranceway that led to the attic.

Grabbing the foldable stairs, he then pulled them down to the floor.

"Wait right here," he told Diamond, who was in a total state of confusion by this time.

"What the hell is he doing?" She thought to herself.

Within minutes, Ceasar was returning.

Diamond could hear his footsteps above her as he approached the attic access door from where he had disappeared.

Caesar reappeared.

When he did return from climbing down the stairs, he was covered in dust. Diamond saw that he was carrying a super heavy-duty trash bag filled to the top with a tiny knot, keeping whatever was in the bag from spilling out.

"Help me carry this to the kitchen," he told her, sounding out of breath.

"Damn, what's in here... a body?" She asked, damn near serious.

After reaching the kitchen, Ceasar untied the bag and began to pull out the things that would eventually change their lives forever.

Then, upon emptying the whole bag out on the table, he saw that there were 10 kilos of cocaine and fifteen pounds of high-grade *Hydro* marijuana, and now, for the first time, he finally realized what it was that was in the bottom of the bag…$70,000 in hundred-dollar bills.

Damn!!!

Both of their eyes had lit up like the midnight sky on the fourth of July at the sight of all that money. And all that either one of them could say was…

"Wow…"

6

CEASAR

"Ceasar Andrews, you have a visit in booth 7," the voice on the intercom had blared.

Waking up from his nap, Ceasar quickly brushed his teeth and put on the county-issued black and white jumper that was assigned to him.

It was only his second day in jail, and he was already dreading waking up in this place.

When he reached the booth that he was designated, he could see Rico through the window of the door.

Ceasar became temporarily at ease seeing his childhood friend come to see him.

Grabbing a seat on a metal stool that was permanently affixed to the jail's concrete floor, Caesar picked up the phone that was used to talk as he watched Rico stare back at him through the thickness of the visitation room glass.

"What's the word, bird," Ceasar began as always.

"Man, everything is everything," Rico answered, "... what da fuck happened, bro? Run me down through there."

The story began...

"I had came from the room fucking wit that freak Tory, right? Deon was blowing me up talking about them *bo's*, so I go to drop 'em to him. You know Amber usually handle all that shit for me, but she wasn't answering, so I get rolled on my way to the nigga."

Rico was shaking his head... "Damn, so what is Frank talking about?" He asked.

Caesar answered him.

"He's going to try to get them to reinstate me; if not, I'm looking at five non-agg."

Rico was still shaking his head.

"Nigga don't need no time right now, bro. So what's da plan ?" He asked Ceasar.

"Shiddd..." Ceasar said, dropping his head, "I need you to run shit for me while I'm gone."

"Chill out, bro. You act like you bout to go sit down or do a bid or sumn. You know Frank gone get you back out to these streets, Dawg."

"Nah, fam, I'm tired of this probation shit hanging over my head. I'm gone take this lil five-piece, sit my ass down right quick, and come back home. I just need you to take my position and hold it down. Diamond gonna introduce you to all the connects and give you the key to the network. All I ask is that you keep the books straight, communicate with me, and look after D. That's it. We good?"

Rico began to assure him.

"Bro, you know if I ain't let you down this far, then I got you. Are you sure that this is what you wanna do?"

Ceasar looked Rico square in the eyes and replied, "Positive."

The day had gone by slowly. Ceasar had started his routine by working out with a Muslim guy named Rasheed.

Most of the time, they would just sit and go back and forth, spitting wisdom.

His day would consist of waking up around 8 am to work out, then shower, then reading as much as possible.

Watching TV wasn't much of his thing, seeing that he didn't really like coming out of his cell.

The first morning that he was actually able to make commissary, he loaded up on as much food and snacks as possible.

Eating jail trays and jail food made him sick to his stomach just thinking about what was in them.

Sometimes, he would just lay back in his bunk, meditating on his plans and how he would break the news to Diamond that he was going to take a five-year sentence this time.

In the back of his mind, he knew she wouldn't be able to handle it. Over time, he just hoped that she would be able to adjust to the situation until he came home. The money wasn't the problem; it was the fact that she was able to keep control of the network.

That's what worried Ceasar.

Men don't take too kindly to having a woman in charge, running the show, and telling them what to do.

Then it hit him... *"Rico."*

Rico could pose as the head of the network, and *she* could just run things from behind the scenes. The only question was...could Rico continue to be loyal to him after seeing so much power?

But only time could tell. Everything was already taking its course.

The next morning came so fast that Ceasar didn't even realize he had fallen asleep.

They were already calling guys out for a visit by the time that he had awakened and showered.

Thirty minutes into a conversation with Rasheed, Ceasar heard his name through the loudspeaker, indicating that he had a visit.

When he walked into the booth, he noticed Diamond sitting in the window... head down, dressed in all black with shades covering her eyes.

"Hey, Baby Girl," Ceasar started, catching her off guard.

"Hey, my love. How are you holding up in this shit hole? I know they ain't feeding you worth shit in here," Diamond replied, taking off her shades, exposing that she clearly had been crying.

"I'm good, baby. The question is... how are you holding up?"

Ceasar mentioned to her that it looked like she had been crying.

"Just my allergies," she lied, "I really have been missin' you like crazy, though. Rico told me how you got pulled over and shit."

Caesar slightly nodded his head, "... yeah. That was some real live bull shit. You told me about that driving and texting shit."

"OK... so I talked to Frank, and he said that he can have you out and reinstated in no time. So the question is, when do you wanna come home?"

"I'm not," Ceasar answered matter of factly without missing a beat.

"Wait... what?" Diamond asked, raising up and straightening her back, "I *know* that I must be tripping because I thought I just heard you say *you're not*."

"Baby, I'm gonna take a five-year plea and do my time. I can't afford to keep walking around with this ten-year probation over my head doing what we do. If I take the five now, I will be out in no time. It's non-aggravated time."

"Ceasar fuck that time! We need you out here! We need you! Don't do this to us, please. Baby, not now," Diamond pleaded as she began to cry uncontrollably, causing her body to shake like crazy.

"Wait a minute... *US?*" Ceasar asked, "What are you talking about? Slow down and breathe. Who is *US?*"

"Us," Diamond said, adding some simple mathematics to it, "As in one plus one equals three.

Ceasar, I'm two months pregnant, according to the doctor."

She dropped her head, "I was gonna wait to surprise you, but now I feel like it's more of an important time to tell you."

Ceasar was happy and confused all at the same time. He really didn't know how to feel at this moment, but he tried to stay in good cheer even though his mind was already made.

"So I'm gonna be a daddy? Awww shit," Ceasar said.

He couldn't have been happier and grief-stricken at the same time if he had even wanted to.

"Look, I'll take this up with Frank and see what we can do," Diamond added without wanting to sound any parts of being disrespectful.

"Let me handle Frank," Ceasar told her, "But in the meantime, I need you to start making the transition and introduce Rico to everybody. It's time."

Ceasar added, "But listen, never give him all the power. You must stay a few steps ahead of the game, baby. Remember…if sumn don't feel right, it *ain't* right. You feel me?"

Diamond nodded her head, "Yes… but baby, why are you talking like this? You're coming home."

"Just listen to me. No matter what happens… I love you."

"I love you too, Ceaz."

Ceasar kissed his two pointer fingers and placed them on the glass. And then made an exit, leaving her there in the booth.

On his way back to his cell, he walked head down with so much on his mind.

"Heavy is the head..." Ceasar thought to himself.

Ceasar had never expected to receive such life-changing information as what Diamond had just laid on him. This changed the situation dramatically, but he still knew that there was nothing he could do but get this time behind him.

When arriving back in his cell, instead of continuing his daily routine, he figured that it was time to kick his plan into action, starting with a letter.

Dear Love,
If you are reading this, then that means I have already signed for five years.
Frank will answer any questions you may have about my release.
First, I wanna let you know that I love you and my seed more than life itself, and in the future, I hope you will understand my reason for taking my time.
I will be releasing my property to you, so please come get it and follow my directions carefully. The storage key on my key ring is never to be given to Rico, but he is free to run through as much work as possible. I want you to call up a network meeting inviting all the bosses and their right-hand men down to brief them on the situation.
Everyone is to answer Rico, and he is to answer you.
No one is to know about our main stash house, I mean.
NOBODY.

If shit gets out of hand, use the red line phone, and you know who to call.
I'm trusting you to stay down for me, but I'm not expecting you to stop living just because I'm gone.
No matter what, I will always love you.

Ceasar
The World Is Yours.

7

DIAMOND

After the letter...

Reading the last few words of Ceasar's letter, Diamond couldn't help but feel lost and alone. It had been two weeks since she visited him, and here she was, reading a letter saying that he had signed for his time. The five years.

Her life began to flash before her eyes at that very moment, which was back to the morning when their lives had changed forever.

That morning after opening the bag...

"D!... D!... Diamond, snap out of it," Ceasar said, nudging her out of her blank stare.

"Huh?… oh, oh yeah, my bad. How did you, I mean, where did you get all of this?" She asked.

"Really, it was a gift from my uncle. But it came with the price of his life."

Ceasar couldn't help but shake his head, thinking about the day that he had lost his Uncle Charles.

"So, what's the plan?" Diamond asked, still in amazement, "You got enough weight here to sew up the city if you do it right."

Ceasar was slow to answer…

"I don't know," he told her, "I mean, the weed is nothing to me. I can handle that… and Melvin knows all the smokers. But the bricks? I ain't never seen so much of it at one time."

"Look, I can help you, but all I ask is that you always look out for me. My twin cousins Keon and Deon live down in Louisiana, and that's all they fuck wit *is* work."

"Bet, but there's one thing," Ceasar explained to her, "We gotta follow the rules of the game. I want you to take the car, go to the bookstore, and pick up all the urban novels you can find. We are both young, and we have a lot to learn about the dope game. I would rather be ahead of the game than to get caught up on some shit that could have been avoided."

Ceasar picked up one of the rubber-banded stacks, slid out a few hundred-dollar bills, and handed them to her before he began speaking again.

"Call your people while you're out and see what's good on their end. One more thing, Diamond," he paused, "Loyalty is everything."

Diamond nodded her head and then leaned over to kiss him on the cheek, replying, "Likewise," as she walked out of the house.

When Diamond returned, she called Ceasar on his

cell phone and asked him to help her with the bags in the car. As she parked, she could see both Melvin and him walking out of the house toward the car.

"Damn, D... what you do, buy the whole store?" Ceasar asked her.

Melvin hadn't said a word yet.

"Well, hello to you too, Melvin. But, if you should know, *Ceasar*, I got the best books I could find. Rubber bands, baggies, scales, extra trac phones, and a lil sumn to cook."

"That's what I'm talkin' about," Melvin said jokingly to his friend Ceasar, "Looks like you got you one, boy."

As Ceasar began to separate the books from the supplies that Diamond had brought back, one particular book caught his attention... *La Costa Nostra.*

"Aye, D..." he started, "Gone ahead and start that food up; me and Melvin bout to crack open a few of these books. Did you holla at yo kinfolk about the issue?"

"Yeah. They're gonna come up here next week to talk numbers and check out the quality."

"Aight," he told her just as Melvin had begun to interrupt their conversation.

"Ceaz, let me ask you sumn," Melvin said, bringing all the attention to himself before continuing, "Why in da hell are we reading these books? We don't need to be in no books; we need to be in da streets."

He sounded aggravated.

Ceaz explained.

"Look... at the level that we're coming into da game,

we ain't like none of these street nigga's. We coming in as *BOSSES.*"

Ceasar continued… "Instead of learning from our mistakes, we gone bypass all that by learning from the mistakes of these niggas in these books."

"Man, I got all the game," Melvin joked, imitating Craig off of the movie *Friday.*

"You might do, but we need to know how to last in the game. If we do this right, we shouldn't ever fall off… ever."

*****

"Diamond," there was a pause.

"Diamond," someone said again.

It was Angie waving her hand in front of Diamond's eyes, trying to catch her attention.

She wasn't sure what the problem was, but tears were streaming down her homegirl's face.

"He's gone. He took the time, Angie. How could he do this to me after all we've been through?"

Angie didn't really know what to say. But she tried, "I know, D… but there got to be a reason behind it all. He wouldn't just leave you for nothing. He loves you, and now that you carrying his seed, I'm sure he loves you even more."

Diamond wiped her eyes, taking a second to clear her mind. It had only been a weekend, but she was already feeling the pain of his absence. No one could ever take the place of Ceasar. He was all she had known since the age of 17.

He had not only left her in charge of a well-known drug organization, but she was now responsible for raising their child.

At a time like this, she couldn't help but want to get away, but she also knew this wasn't the time to break down and let all of their hard work go down the drain.

Pregnant or not, it was now time to kick it up a notch and put Ceasar's plan into action… and it started with one phone.

A phone call to Rico.

It was early Friday morning when Diamond decided to meet with Rico at their compound on the west side of Dallas.

The compound was an old storage warehouse that Ceasar had purchased to store the cars that he used for transporting his product and also as a place to hold his important meetings.

Diamond had chosen this location so they could talk in-depth about the network's future plans without running the risk of having any extra ears in their conversation.

Pulling into the gate of the property, Diamond was escorted by a caravan of her own bodyguards. Two armed men were driving her in a black tinted-out SUV, and two armed men behind her were driving the same type of vehicle.

After entering the garage, the two trucks parked parallel to each other and killed their engines.

As the first two guys got out, they noticed Rico approaching in his white 420 Benz.

Rico always chose to ride in style when he was handling business. It came with the territory.

After seeing Rico exit the car, Diamond signaled for her bodyguards to let her out.

"I'm glad you could meet me at such a last minute, bro." Diamond began.

"Come on now, sis, you know I got you. You ain't gotta worry about that. Now tell me, what's da plan?" Rico replied, rubbing his hands together.

"Well, Ceasar made it real clear that he wants you to pose as the head of the organization until his return. As for me, I will be running everythang from behind the scenes and communicating with the plugs."

"You know what?... I'm tripping," Rico started, "I've always known that Ceasar *wouldn't* plug me in. But I just figured that since I was his boy that, he would've at least trusted me a little more. Don't take it the wrong way. No pun intended."

"I feel you, Bruh Bruh," Diamond responded, "But this is the way he wants it. But you will be seeing more money then you've ever dreamed about. Are you in?"

Diamond stretched out her hand, signaling for a handshake.

Rico reciprocated the gesture by grabbing her hand, turning it over, and lightly kissing it, signaling his respect and cooperation.

On the way back home, as she reflected on Rico's

initial reaction, something just wasn't sitting right with her about it.

She had never expected him to have that type of outburst after she told him the plan.

This gave her a terrible feeling about what was to come.

Diamond had always gone with her gut feelings in the game, and today, her gut was telling her to put a damage control plan into action.

Ring

Ring

"Talk to me, bitch," she heard her homegirl say.

"Angie, meet me at the crib in 30 minutes. I need you… code PINK."

And that was all she had to say.

"I'm on my way," Angie ended, and the phone went dead.

The ringing of the doorbell snapped Diamond from a daydream again, signaling that Angie had just arrived.

"Boss, you have a visitor here to see you at the gate. Would you like for me to escort her into the velvet room?" One of her bodyguards asked.

"No, it won't be necessary. Show her to the garden, and I will be out shortly."

The land that this house was sitting on was massive, taking up 5 acres in all.

Full-sized golden gate-style fencing surrounded the entire property, an outpost for the guards to watch the surveillance cameras, and trained guard dogs roaming all over the fence line.

The house was originally built to resemble the White House, not only in looks but particularly in security as well.

Trying to change her mood, Diamond ordered her cook, Gloria, to prepare some drinks and meet her outside.

Taking the elevator down to the ground floor, she could see Angie on the phone as she made her way to the flower garden. As she stepped closer and closer, staying silent, she could now overhear Angie's whole conversation.

"Baby, I told you that I don't know what she's up to, but it's big. I'ma call you soon as I leave, okay? Bye."

"Who was that?" Diamond asked, startling Angie to the point that she even dropped her phone.

"Girl, nobody. Just a lil *bug-a-boo* that won't take a hint. What's up with this code pink shit? I need all the details on this one."

"We gone talk about that at the meeting tonight," Diamond told her, "Right now, I just wanna get a couple of these drinks in me and kick back with my bitch."

Diamond then took a sip out of one of the glasses that Gloria had brought and passed Angie the other one.

The next hour had gone by so quickly that the girls didn't even notice that the sun had started to set, causing the sky to give off an orangish hue.

Diamond had planned to meet with the network the following day when all of the members had arrived in town. As far as she was concerned, time was ticking, and she needed to take the rest of the day to be to herself, collect her thoughts, and prepare for tomorrow.

She decided to end the visit.

"Damn, I didn't even notice that it was getting so late. Angie, I've got a few things to take care of. We're gonna have to get together early tomorrow or something."

Angie wasn't tripping about it.

"It's cool; I gotta run a few errands anyway. Get at me in the a.m..... cool?"

Diamond agreed, leaning in and giving her a hug, kissing her on the cheek.

She then added, "Angie, no matter what, I will always love you, girl."

"Gurl, chill... you act like you ain't gone see me tomorrow."

Angie made her exit.

Instead of walking through the house to the front door, Angie had decided to take the sidewalk that led around the side of the house to the front driveway where her car was parked.

Watching Angie from her upstairs office, Diamond could see her white Lexus exit out of the gate and disappear out of sight.

Ring

Ring

"Yes, Boss Lady," Blue answered.

"Clip that bitch."

Diamond's voice was strong and demanding. But

her face showed something otherwise as one lone single tear fell from her eye.

Diamond had just ordered two of her closest hitmen to follow Angie and end her life.

As Angie turned right onto Ledbetter, she noticed a black Chevy Tahoe truck jump two lanes over in order to make the same turn that she had made.

"Hmmm," she thought to herself.

To make sure that she wasn't jumping to conclusions, Angie decided to make another quick right on the following street.

Seeing the SUV make the same exact turn *again* had sent her mind into a frenzy, causing her heart to beat triple time.

Reaching under the driver's seat, she located the chrome 9mm handgun that she purchased previously when she and Diamond had made one of their weekly trips to the gun range.

She pulled the car over to the side of the road and slammed on the brakes.

Angie made an attempt to crawl over the armrest and out the passenger side door.

Right before she could exit the car, she could hear the sound of two automatic rifles spraying the car from front to back. Angie's mind was racing. Before she could fully exit, one of the bullets from the gunman ripped through her shoulder and sent her tumbling to the pavement.

The gunfire ceased, and Angie could hear the footsteps of the assassins approaching her.

Trying to reach for her weapon, she saw two masked men enter her view, which was now beginning to blur.

"Check, mate," whispered one of the men.

Before taking her last breath, Angie spat blood onto one of the men's shoes and then replied, "Fuck you!!!… and tell Diamond that I said I'ma die a real bitch!!!"

Angie was finishing her last words just as the hitmen had begun loading round after round into her body until they felt that their job was done.

And it was.

Lifeless, Angie's body lay there in the street. Bloody, riddled with bullets, both eyes open, face to the sky.

If only she had remained true to the game.

8

DIAMOND

Back at the mansion, the driveway was filling up with all types of luxury cars, signaling that the network was arriving.

Diamond had arranged for the meeting to begin an hour later, but almost everyone was already in attendance.

Amongst the crowd, she could see her twin cousins, Keon and Deon, making their way to the area where she was seated.

"Wazzam, D?" Her cousin Keon asked her, "Tell me sumn good, gangsta."

"Shit, Kee. A bitch just been taking da good wit da bad tryna keep my head above water. How's everything back home?"

He answered, "Same ol two step... just a different song. I heard about Ceasar. If you need us in town for a while, just let me know."

Deon stepped into the conversation, picking up on her change of mood. Depressing.

"D, you know that this shit is part of the game. It comes with it. Don't let the situation get the best of you," he told her.

"I'm good. Soon as Rico gets here, we can get this show on the road. Dude should have been pulled up already, though."

Just as she finished her sentence, she could see Rico entering the room with two of his young workers from the southside.

This was the day that she was supposed to brief the network on the sudden changes and introduce Rico to the head position.

It was a task that she was starting to regret more and more each and every time that he showed his face.

From where she was standing, it appeared that everyone had arrived. The room had become packed, and all of the lieutenants and generals were surrounded by their soldiers, creating different sections in the room.

Now being ready to begin, Diamond signaled for Rico to come take his place at her side.

Rico came up, "What up, lil sis?... you ready to get this show on the road?"

"Yeah, just let me do all the talking so I can try to walk everybody through the specifics and shit."

"Hey… you the boss," he told Diamond.

Grabbing her champagne glass, Diamond took a spoon and began tapping it at the side, letting everybody know to take their position at the round table.

"Alright, men... I'm sure that all of you are wondering what's the purpose of this meeting and where Ceasar is. Just last week, Ceaz signed for a five-year non-aggravated sentence in hopes of coming back home in at least a year or two."

As she was finishing that very sentence, the room became filled with whispers and different discussions between the groups, which, within seconds, created a loud outburst of questioning and concerns.

"Gentlemen! Gentlemen!" Diamond said, raising her voice to regain control of the room before adding, "... look, there is no need for panic. We still got the keys to the city, and with the right plan, we take this shit to a whole 'nother level. I want everybody to be playing with M's in six month's time. But in order to do that, we gotta tighten up."

Standing to his feet, Zo, *the general representing Arkansas*, began to question the move.

"Wait a minute," he began, "so my nigga Ceaz is locked up for a five-year stretch, and I'm just supposed to fall in line with his chick? Man, I put too much work into this shit to be led by somebody who don't know half the shit that comes with these streets."

Diamond took that as a straight offense.

"Nigga, I been in these streets, and I'ma die in these streets," she told him and everybody else who was listening, "There ain't shit under the sun that I ain't seen, so get with the program or get cut the fuck off. It's *that* simple, nigga. Is that understood?"

There was complete silence as Zo retreated back to his seat and sat his fat ass down.

No one spoke.

Weird.

The network was used to seeing her as a quiet, polite type who stayed on Ceasar's side and never said anything. They had never experienced this side of the Diamond that stood before them tonight.

"Now, I would like to introduce all of you to Rico. Ceasar's best friend and my right hand."

Standing to his feet, Rico gave a slight head nod and took the floor, giving his introduction into what he'd liked to call "New Work."

His speech was short but directly to the point, showing everyone that he meant business. Whatever doubts they might have had about this situation in the beginning were erased by the conclusion of his speech.

Diamond respected his poise and ability to lead, but at the end of the day, and in her mind, she still felt that he wasn't to be trusted.

Diamond had begun wrapping things up.

"Well, gentlemen, we all know that Ceasar would never fly y'all all the way out to Texas just to bore you to sleep with business details. We have live entertainment, food, drinks, and more. *Mi casa, su casa,*" she told them, "But everybody must get with me before leaving town to iron out a few wrinkles in the details and to speak on a few specifics."

Everyone agreed with a head nod, signaling the meeting was now over, and the party had begun.

There were women in bikinis, bottles of Ace of Spades, and servants coming from every direction.

When Ceaz was out, he was known for throwing some of the most banging parties for the network. So today would be no exception.

As the festivities began, Diamond left it all in Rico's hands and decided to call it a night.

Usually, she would be right on her man's side, enjoying the dancers along with the rest of the team, but tonight, her emotions were getting the best of her.

Now, as she stood outside the guest house, she could feel herself crumbling to pieces.

It was like her whole world had come crashing down on her like a ton of bricks.

"D, what's up?... you aight?" Her twin cousin Keon had asked her, "I didn't even see you slide out?"

He had stepped out to take a phone call when he noticed her out in the garden.

"I know you ain't gone miss the show? Everybody is looking for you in there," he told her.

"I'm good, Kee," Diamond told him, "I ain't really in the mood."

Keon took a wild guess… "It's about Ceaz, ain't it?"

It was at that moment that Diamond had realized just how transparent she really was.

She stared at her cousin in silence and let him speak.

"On the cool, it's all over ya face, cuzo. But keep your head up, tho'. You know they can't hold a real nigga forever. That jail shit really just a part of the game, so you gotta learn how to roll with the punches."

She continued listening to him...he was making sense.

"Stay focused," he told her, "he'll be home before you know it. Write him, send him pictures and make sure his books *stay* straight. Don't no nigga respect a bitch that won't hold him down. Remember that, you feel me?"

"I got you, kinfolk," Diamond said, suddenly feeling a slight bit better, "Thank you for being here. It's good to see a familiar face around."

Keon had gotten through to her... at least for now. Family sometimes can do that.

But for the moment and the night...

"Shiiddd, who knows...I might be here to stay if one of these strippers put it on me like they say they can. Come on in here and kick it with me one time for the one time, fam."

Diamond thought about it, straightened her shoulders, and brought her perfect smile back to life...

"Fuck it," she said, pushing her worries to the side and putting herself into party character mode, "Let's go turn up then, Kee. We own this city!!!"

9

CEASAR

48, breathe...
49, breathe...
50, breathe...

Ceasar had just finished his last set of push-ups, wrapping up his morning workout routine.

It had been two weeks since he had been transferred to one of the State's most frequently filled prisons…the Middleton unit. This was a processing facility about 300 miles from home in Abilene.

The first day that he arrived at the unit turned out to be more of a test than he had expected it to be. It was more of a degrading process than anything.

He was forced to strip down to nothing alongside 30 other men, and worst of all, he had to shave his head completely bald for the first time in his life.

It had taken him almost 3yrs to grow his dreads to

the length that they were, so when it came time to cut them, he felt as if he was being reduced to nothing.

As the days went by, Ceasar had to adjust to being woken up early in the mornings to attend the processing procedures that he could not escape by any means. Every single prisoner had to go through it.

By the second week, he had adapted to the early schedule and had begun to use it to his advantage.

On this particular morning, after his workout and shower, he chose to sit out in the dayroom to watch TV…something that he normally wouldn't do.

It was early Sunday.

Football had been shown on the sports channel, causing everyone to sit in one area.

The tank or pod, which some may call it, that he had been assigned to was a sixty-man dorm-like living area with bunk beds outlining the entire room. There were seven tables and four benches positioned in the middle of the floor used to view the two flatscreens mounted on the walls above the restrooms.

"You gone come check this game out, nigga?" He was asked, "The Cowboys been killin' something lately."

"Yeah, let me hit da shower right quick and hop fresh, gangsta. I'ma fuck with you in a minute."

When Ceasar arrived on the chain, the first face he recognized was Money… another well-known street cat from his old neighborhood.

Money was a few years younger than Ceasar but had still been in the streets for almost the same amount of time.

They would always cross each other's paths either in the club or while being out at the mall.

Money was raised in Bonton Projects in South Dallas to a family of 10... seven brothers and three sisters.

At an early age, his older brother Sean had given him the game and put him to work by allowing him to sit in one of his local drug houses.

This was basically how his life of crime had begun.

The benches in the dayroom began to fill up as the Cowboys were set to play the Washington Redskins for their season opener.

Most of the other inmates were already placing their bets on the team they felt was going to win.

"What it's lookin' like, Money Man," Caesar yelled.

"Shit, they just now about to kick off. Who you running with, my boy?"

"I put ten mackerel packs down on *Da Boys*," he told him, "You know how I'm rocking, and if anybody else in here wanna buck them Cowboys, put your muthafuckin money where your mouth go!"

Ceasar was yelling, trying to catch the attention of anyone who was willing to bet against him.

"I got five dollars that dem Cowgirls don't do shit, straight up! Sanchez, one of the Hispanic guys on the front row, challenged."

"Make that twenty dollars, and we got a deal," Caesar says, accepting the challenge.

The game had started off slow. Both teams failed to

score, which resulted in them punting the ball back and forth.

By mid-second quarter, the Cowboys had gained momentum, scoring 17 unanswered points.

Ceasar and Money were talking cash shit every time they made a play by jumping out of their seats, slapping high fives, and taunting the guys they had placed a bet with.

At the end of the game, they had been yelling so much that both of them were hoarse and could barely speak without their voice cracking.

The final score was Cowboys 27... Redskins 13.

Josh, the first guy Ceasar had placed a bet with, had dumped the ten meat packs onto the table where both Money and Ceaz had been sitting after the game was over.

Hours had passed since the game had gone off, but Sanchez was still walking around bullshitting like he didn't have a debt to pay.

Caesar was beginning to get upset.

"What's up with this nigga steady walking around this hoe like he don't owe me no money, lil bro? I damn near forgot we had a bet. It's been so long. He must think that I'm a hoe or sumn," Caesar said, wondering if by not paying him, the guy thought that he was weak.

Was he testing Ceasar's manhood?

"Just chill, Ceaz," Money had told him, "Dude might have forgot or sumn. Plus, you know you don't need to be getting into no shit at all right now. You gotta try to make parole. Them streets need you, G. But if the nigga wanna take it there, you know that I'm rockin' with you."

"I just hate when somebody knows damn well that they owe you, but they wanna pay up the money on *their* damn time. I bet if the shoe was on the other foot, it would be a whole 'nother story. I'ma just go see what's happening though… watch my back," Ceasar replied.

Walking over to the corner where Sanchez's bed was located, Ceasar's blood had begun to boil, but he was doing his best to control his anger.

The corner area where Sanchez's bunk was located was called *"Little Mexico"* because most of the guys who stayed over there were of Hispanic ethnicity.

"Aye, man… let me holla at you about sumn right fast."

Caesar was really cool about it.

"I'm busy right now, migo. Come back later, then we talk, wey."

Was he serious?

"Naw, we need to talk now," Caesar told him, "We need to talk *right* now. I ain't with that later shit, fam."

"You run nothing here. I say you lower your tone and go back over to the ghetto like a good little boy. Wait for me to come get at you. Huh, homeboy?"

Caesar was actually getting tired of talking and going back and forth about something behind some money that rightfully belonged to him.

"I don't know who the fuck you think your talkin' to, homeboy… but I'm not your bitch or your podna.

Just pay me what you owe, and we won't have to get into no gangsta shit in here."

As Ceasar's voice became louder, you could feel the tension between the blacks and Hispanics grow.

There was a crowd beginning to form in the corner where they were as they were now standing face to face.

Just as blows were about to be exchanged, one of the guards who was assigned to the floor walked in to do a routine count.

"Count time!" The guard shouted.

The guard could tell that something was going on.

"Alright, guys, break it up. There's nothing to see here. Come on, on your bunks before you do something all y'all going to regret."

The crowd was now starting to lighten up, leaving them in an intense stare-down that neither guy wanted to be the first to back down on.

Defusing the situation, Money wrapped his arm around Ceasar's neck, leading him back into their area for count time.

At this point, he was boiling.

Without even knowing it, Ceasar was pacing back and forth, keeping his eye trained on Sanchez's every move.

"Bro, calm down. We gone handle that shit. We just gotta catch him when the guards ain't watching."

"Fuck all that. The next time I get close enough to that nigga…I'm taking off. Guard or no guard."

"It don't matter, G. However you wanna rock, I'm rollin' with you regardless."

"Bet," Caesar told him.

The next day seemed to be more tense inside the dorm.

Everyone was on pins and needles, waiting to see how the whole situation would play out.

But these were the type of moments that Ceasar thrived on, and he knew that there would be no better time to strike than the present.

Around noon, when it was time for everyone to line up to go to the chow hall, both Ceasar and Money hopped in the back of the same line Sanchez was in.

Halfway to the chow hall, he noticed them trailing in the same line, just a few people behind him.

Sanchez was also walking with two guys from his hometown, whom he had informed about the altercation that happened the night before.

Inside the chow hall, Ceasar chose to sit a few tables down from where Sanchez and his people were seated.

There was one guard positioned by the entrance door and another whose job was to get the inmates in and out of the chow hall in seven-minute intervals.

Just as the guard who was walking the floor stepped out the door to check traffic, Ceasar stepped into action, taking his lunch tray to the back of Sanchez's head.

Money, just as he said that he would do, caught his first target off guard by crashing a thunderous right hook to his jaw, sending him to the concrete floor with a thud.

By this time, Ceasar was going to work landing blow after blow into his defenseless opponent's head and face.

In the aisle of the chow hall, Money was going toe to toe with one of the bigger Hispanics, Pedro.

Pedro stood at 6'4, weighing in at about 240lbs, which gave him more of a size advantage over Money, who was still handling him.

Ducking two sloppy punches, Money quickly came back at him with a flashing uppercut, sending Pedro stumbling a few steps.

After regaining himself, Pedro charged him with the force of a wild man and grabbed him into a deadly bear hug. The pressure of Pedro's arms was beginning to squeeze the life out of Money. He could now see guards starting to rush in from every direction, but he was still beginning to slip out of consciousness.

Out of nowhere, he could see Ceasar cocking back and delivering a powerful right hook to Pedro from Pedro's blindside.

Ceasar's blow caused Pedro to release him, sending his head crashing into the pavement.

"Bitch ass nigga," Ceasar had begun to say, but his sentence was cut short by the guards' mase and their billy clubs.

All he could remember was his vision fading to black. When he had come to, he could see nothing but black, and it felt as if he was lying on a cold bed of ice.

It took a second for his vision to regain clear focus, but when it did, he could now tell that he was lying on the floor of a cell in segregation.

As soon as he tried to sit up, he could feel a sharp pain shooting through the small of his back. It turned out that the special response team had beaten both Ceasar and Money until they collapsed on the floor and then drugged them into different cells in the *Seg* building.

"Aye, Money!... Money!" Caesar yelled out, searching for his homeboy.

"Yeah!" His homie Money answered.

"You good, fam?"

"Hell naw...I can't see outta my right eye, nigga. They fucked me up a lil bit, Bruh, Bruh."

"Damn," Ceasar told him, "We gone be aight though. Money, I like the way you handled yourself back there on some G shit. When we get back to the world, I got you, and that's my word."

"I got you, O.G."

After that, Ceasar adjusted himself on the cold floor to try to be as comfortable as possible...considering, and went back to sleep.

10

———

RICO

"Let me see these in size 10 1/2".

Rico had been in the Galleria Mall for the past hour, looking for something to wear to the grand opening of a new upscale nightclub called *Chocolate City*.

Everybody was supposed to be in the building tonight for an album release party that he was throwing for one of his up-and-coming Conrads, who was under his rap label... *Stretched Out Records*.

Rico had been getting calls all day from multiple people asking about getting in free and the going price of the *VIP* sections.

"Would you like a glass of champagne while you are waiting?" One of the women working the floor asked as she made her rounds checking on the customers.

She was a short, brown-skinned girl with a short, wavy hairdo.

Her eyes were of a light hazel color that squeenched like an angel at him, giving them a soft bedroom look.

Following her perfect C-cup size breast to her slim waistline with his eyes, he couldn't help but notice the roundness of the girl's backside.

"I'll tell you what I *would* like," Rico said in a seductive tone.

"And what might that be?" She asked.

"Your name, number, address, email, and however else I might be able to reach you for dinner tomorrow night."

The girl replied with a light chuckle.

"Well, my name is Melody, but my friends call me Mel, and I don't just hand out my number to random guys that I meet at work."

"Well, I'm Rico, and I don't just *normally* try to talk to women who I meet in the shoe department, but when I see sumptin I like…I just go for it."

"Is that right, Tiger?"

"Tiger?" He laughed. "The name is Rico, and yes, that is right. But here, take my number and call me sometime. Maybe we can have lunch one day soon, on me."

Rico assumed that he had delivered his line smoothly as he tried passing her a business card that had his number printed on it.

"Okay, Mr. Rico," the girl whose name was Melody was saying while taking the card but casually denying the lunch offer, "maybe I will, maybe I won't."

Rico looked at her before she walked away. After the

clerk returned with the correct shoe size, he made his purchase and headed toward the exit. On the way out, he made it his business to walk past Mel one last time.

"Maybe you will, maybe you want," he whispered to her as he exited.

She watched him walk out, leaving a trail of very nice-smelling cologne.

*****

Remembering getting slapped.

"There dat fuck nigga go right there walking out of the mall. Trying to shine like everything's all good around this bitch."

Chase scoffed as he continued hitting a blunt of *Kush* weed before passing it back to his little flunkie… A-Wall.

Ever since the day that Rico had gone off and slapped him on the spot, he had sworn on his mother's grave that he would make him pay.

It made him feel more played than *anything* to be slapped.

"This is what I want you to do," Chase was telling A-Wall, "Pull around to the front of the mall as he's walkin' out… then, keep a slow, steady speed."

"Bet, I got you, big bro. You know I'm down for the cause," A-Wall replied as he began to exit the parking lot and pull around to the front entrance of the mall.

Chase checked the twin chrome Rugars to make sure they were cocked and off safely.

Coming to a slow crawl, Chase let down the passenger window and climbed up onto the car door, positioning himself to where he was leaning over the top of the car, guns aimed at Rico.

Just as he had begun pulling the trigger, he could see a younger female pushing Rico out of the way, causing one of the bullets to strike her in the chest.

Chase could see a crowd going into pandemonium.

There was glass shattering and sparks flying everywhere.

He was trying his hardest to fix his aim on Rico, who was now crawling towards the girl.

"Go, go, go!" Chase screamed, "Damn man, what the fuck?"

"What's up, bro? You hit da nigga? What happened?"

"Hell naw, fuck! We gone have to put some more work in. You down?" He asked his driver.

"And you know it," A-Wall answered, locking himself in.

After seeing the black SUV speed off, Rico could hear the cries of different mall goers who were affected by the drive-by.

Their eyes finally started to rest on the woman who had pushed him out of the way of the attack. And then, as he, too, looked closer, it hit him. It was Melody. Melody had just saved his life.

"Melody!" He yelled, "Mel... stay with me, baby girl! Help is on the way. Somebody call 911, hurry up! Get us some help!"

"It burns, Rico. Pl... please help me," the girl that he had just met pleaded.

"Shhh... don't talk. Save your strength; help will be here any minute. Just hold on."

Rico could tell that she was slipping away, but all he could do was continue applying pressure to the wound and try to keep her conscious.

Grabbing her hand, he saw a piece of paper. A piece of paper that she had been carrying at the time of the shooting. He unfolded it.

It read…

Melody
214-555-0139
I guess I will

At that moment, he realized that she would always be more than just another chick that he ran into at the mall.

She had just risked everything to save his life.

After getting Mel stabilized and stitched up, the doctors put her under close supervision for her recovery.

The bullet had missed her lung by an inch, which allowed them to extract it quite easily.

She was still heavily sedated by the time they let Rico in to see her, so all he could do was sit and wait. After being in and going through such a traumatizing and close-to-death situation, he decided not to attend the night's party. It would also serve and be considered more as a security hazard than anything.

It wouldn't be smart nor safe to be in the club with such a big ass X on his back at this time.

Instead, he decided to call up a meeting amongst himself and his close teammates to get down to the bottom of this.

What the hell is going on?

First, it was Angie.

Now, someone had attempted to take his life in broad daylight.

Rico was beginning to think that Diamond and the network had something to do with it and that they were behind this whole fiasco.

The meeting was set to take place around 7:30 pm, so he still had enough time to make a few stops before it began.

Before leaving the hospital, he made sure to fill Mel's room with as many flowers and balloons as possible, just in case she awakened while he was away. He left, glad as hell that she had made it through.

When he arrived at the meeting, every single one of his soldiers was already seated at the round table waiting for him to enter.

He had made it a point to stay in the same bloody clothes that he had been in all day.

It added more drama to the situation.

As he walked into the room, the noise turned into an eerie silence, which changed the mood.

The atmosphere was thick with anticipation.

Everybody was trying to figure out if Rico had been shot, and if not…where did all this blood come from?

Seating himself at the head of the table, Rico could see that all eyes were on him and that he had everyone's undivided attention.

Everyone was now anticipating his words. Instead of *trying* to figure out exactly what was going on, they wanted to hear it straight from the horse's mouth.

"First, I would like to inform you that this is not *my* blood. It's the blood of an innocent bystander, which should not have happened."

He continued, "Today, as I was leaving the mall, I was the target of a drive-by. As soon as the first shot went off, I was pushed out of the way by a young woman who didn't deserve to be the victim of my beef. I believe that I know who was behind this attack, but first, I gotta do my homework to make sure that I'm right.

The tension in the room became thick, causing one of the soldiers, Rich, to stand up and interrupt Rico's speech.

"Fuck that, bruh! I say we just get out here and start lighting shit up. Fuck the whole damn city up!"

Murmurs started in the crowd.

"That's why you are not in charge, Rich. There's no logic behind what you saying. That ain't gone bring us any answers. It's just gonna bring us a bunch of heat and a whole lot less money."

Rich was a young hothead who believed in using guns versus using his brain.

Rico had taken him under his wing at the early age of eleven after catching him stealing out of the local *7/Eleven* on Leadbetter.

"I need everybody's ears to the streets," said Rico.

"I want them lil nigga's heads just for thinking something sweet about me…or us," he added.

As he dismissed the meeting, he could see Breanna making her way towards him in such a graceful manner that it was as if time had stopped.

No woman had ever captured his heart the way she had.

Breanna had everything that he could wish for, but they were too much alike… and for this very reason, they both agreed a long time ago to let things be.

"Damn, Rico… why didn't you call me? You know, reinforcements would have been sent in a time like this. Are you hit?" She asked.

"Nah… I'm Gucci. I just got caught in a little crossfire, that's all."

As the conversation continued, the room began to empty out little by little until every member had exited, leaving them completely alone.

Their bodyguards were always taught to secure the perimeter and occupy the vehicle. They both ran the exact same type of operation.

"But look," Rico began telling her, "You know I'm a big boy. I got it all under control."

"You don't know who it was… do you?" Breanna asked with a concerned look on her face.

"Hell the fuck naw," he replied.

Breanna started in, "Look Rico, I know your answer will be the same as always, so I'm not asking you, I'm telling you. I'm leaving a unit here to be an extra force at your disposal. Three of my closest men from B-More have proven their loyalty and collected *many* bodies for me. Okay?" She tried explaining.

"Look, Bre.. I'm good on your little henchmen. I don't need no niggas watching my moves. They just gone be in the way."

"You know I'm just worried about you, right? Seeing all this blood really had your girl shook. I didn't know what to think."

Was Breanna getting emotional?

As she finished her sentence, tears began to fill her eyes, which caused her to instantaneously turn her back to Rico.

"Look, I understand this whole situation, and I know you wanna be here for me, but I'm good, Bre. I have two of my best men on top of this shit as we speak."

As Rico spoke, she could feel the warmth of his breath on the back of her neck, causing a slight moisture between her legs.

Before she knew it, he had his manhood pressed against her ass and was wrapping both of his arms firmly around her.

Just as much as she would have loved for him to bend her over and slide into her already wet crevice, she knew Rico wanted the same.

But as he had turned her around to kiss her, one of

her guards had walked in, catching them at an awkward time.

Startled, Bre moved and created a weird but clear distance between them away from Rico.

"Charles, we're done here," Breanna ordered, "Grab the truck and inform the men to be out front in 5 minutes exactly."

"Yes, Ma'am," Charles replied, stopping abruptly and turning around to exit the same door that he had just walked through.

"Damn, Shawty," Rico giggled kind of, "You got these niggas trained, huh?"

Breanna shot back, "Hey, I learned from the best, didn't I?"

"Look, I need to be getting back. When are you leaving town?" Rico asked her.

"Tomorrow… maybe we can link up before I go?"

"We'll see, love… bang my line," he told her.

He loved playing hard to get with Bre. It made their encounters that much more exciting.

11

DIAMOND

It was approximately 4:44 am, and Diamond had been tossing and turning all night, trying to get some sleep.

As she rolled back over to what was usually Ceasar's side of the bed, she saw a shadow-like figure standing near the window.

The glare from the window created a silhouette of what looked to be Ceasar.

"I told you that I would never leave your side, no matter what. Remember?" The figure said.

"I know, baby. It's just with everything that's going on, I feel so lost. Nothing even makes sense anymore," Diamond answered.

"D, you got this. You helped me build this shit play-by-play, and if it wasn't for you,

there wouldn't even be a network. Don't ever let these nigga's see you sweat."

Ring

Ring

"Huh?"

Diamond realized she had dozed off after being awakened by the phone.

"Talk to me," she answered.

"Boss Lady… we're having a situation down at the warehouse. You might wanna get down here," Ron spilled into the phone.

The warehouse.

Ron happened to be one of the head lieutenants in charge of running the distribution warehouse. As Diamond walked through the warehouse corridor led by him and his conrad J.C., another one of her closest lieutenants, Diamond could hear the screaming of what sounded like a man begging and pleading for his life.

"Please, please… I promise that I ain't had nothing to do with it, Rico. You gotta believe me, please!" The man yelled.

Diamond walked in shouting… "Rico! What the fuck going on in here?"

"This motherfucka killed Angie Diamond! … and now he's gotta die! "I don't give a fuck," Rico spat, slapping the shit out of the guy once more.

"Wait, wait, wait! How the fuck do you know that he killed Angie?" Ron asked.

"Look! His girl had on Angie's *Rolex* that I bought her for her birthday!" Rico replied, still yelling.

He looked through his pockets to fetch a bloody gold watch to pass over to Diamond.

Diamond looked at it.

"What the hell is this Rico?"

"His bitch blood! I killed that lil bitch too!"

Diamond looked at the watch and then at the guy who now seemed to have a stare on his face that could break any human person's heart by the sheer look of fear that was in his eyes.

He tried to speak…

"Diamond, please tell him I bought that from…"

Damn!!!

Before the young guy could speak another mumbling word, Diamond had silenced him with a bullet to the head.

"D… what the fuck, man!" Rico shouted angrily, "The nigga was just about to give up the info!"

Diamond was clever, though...

"Man, you should have been done killed this nigga. You already done shot his bitch!"

Rico tried to calm his words...

"D, the nigga kept saying that the only person that he would talk to was you. I was trying to get a name."

Diamond held her ground...

"Fuck, I look like coming all the way down here to talk? Nigga, I thought I was doing you a favor."

Rico stepped in a little closer just so that their conversation remained only within earshot of each other.

"First, Angie got shot at, then *I* get shot at, and now you kill *this* nigga before spilling the info?"

"Wait... what? You got shot at?" Diamond asked, clearly surprised.

"When was this?" She asked.

"When was this?" Rico laughed, mocking her, "... last week leaving the mall. Don't act like you don't know this."

And she didn't...

"Bro, this my first time even hearing some shit like that, Rico. On me," she swore.

"Yeah…aight, D. I gotcha."

The look in Rico's eyes was a burning but cold stare.

"J.J., Malik… let's roll," Rico shouted as he and his men exited the east corridor of the building.

"Somebody clean this shit up," Diamond shouted before leaving herself.

A heavy wind was blowing through the streets of Downtown Dallas, causing Diamond's *Burberry* Fall edition trench coat to sway as she entered a local coffee shop on the south end of Lamar, the city's newly renamed *Botham Jean Blvd.*

This was a regular meet-up spot where she and Caesar usually met to connect.

Making her way through an empty aisle, she could see Jose already sitting at a table in the far right corner.

He was accompanied by two giant bodyguards that resembled the type that you see in those Russian movies.

Before having a seat across from him, Diamond had passed a medium-sized duffle bag to one of the guards, signifying the network's payment.

"Hola," Ms. Diamond said, "So happy to have you join us tonight. I'm sorry to hear what happened with Ceasar. But he is a very smart man; he will figure this out.

"Wait... you already know what happened with Ceaz? How?" Diamond asked in amazement.

Jose raised his hand, signaling for her to stop speaking.

"Listen, Diamond. The problem isn't how do I know. The problem is with Ceasar out of the picture right now. What ensures me that business will continue without a hinge or glitch? You have a lot of hungry wolves over there. No?"

Diamond looked at him with a straight face.

"Jose, I'm not going to lie to you. When I received the news, it fucked me up just like it would do any man's wife. That's because I am a woman before anything. Being a woman at the top of a man's game presents its own challenges, but you gotta remember... I've been on Ceasar's side from day one. Play for play. He probably wouldn't even be hustling if it wasn't for us building that solid foundation together. So, with all due respect, Jefe, I think that today's payment was more than enough proof that I got things under control."

"This may be true. But only time will tell, Senorita Andrews. Until then, I will be holding back a quarter of your supply as a little insurance," he told her.

"Insurance? Come on, Jefe... *money* is insurance. You know I got this all under control. I just left the meeting with our network, and everything looks to be smooth as a baby's bottom."

She continued on as she played a video of the Networks meeting on her phone.

All that could be seen was each member exiting, kissing her ring, and paying their respects as they left.

"It's always been loyalty over everything with us," she told Jose, "My husband taught us best."

Jose took a long pause and stared deep into her eyes.

To Diamond, she knew that she had to keep her poker face intact. Ceasar had taught her this *real* early in the game.

Losing Jose's supply would put them in a very bad spot, and without their usual order, some of the states could be looking at being dry for a minute.

Jose spoke...

"Your move with a teammate of someone that I already do business with bothers me. You see, hunger is one thing, but greed is a whole nother different thing. What separates the two? Why not wait until Caesar comes home to continue business?"

Diamond answered... in words that only a true hustler could understand...

"Hunger is the fuel and passion that gives us that perpetual force that propels us towards our goals...yet it still alerts us when we're full."

She continued... "But greed? Greed is a passion with no means of an end...having no morals or remorse of who or what they step on in the pursuit of their own happiness."

There became a respectful silence between the two as Jose slowly and mentally took his time deciphering her words. With an approving nod of his head, he decided that the meeting was over.

"Hmm... well spoken," he said.

Raising to his feet, he told her, "Look, I hold the quarter. That's insurance. Next month, we back to regular business, okay?"

Jose finished as the two bodyguards returned with a set of keys.

These weren't your ordinary set of keys when transporting, and they never met Jefe with any product from him. He would always provide them with a set of keys to four semi-trucks, which would be parked off a pier. But this time, there were only three sets. She wondered about the fourth.

But Jose always tried to stay a few steps ahead of the game.

As Diamond took the keys, she bowed her head to show gratitude.

Jefe disappeared out of the door, and so did she.

"Dominique, take me to the top of this corner," Diamond demanded to her driver after seeing a figure earlier that looked to be Rico coming out of El Jefe's joint.

Was she tripping? Or was it really him?

Diamond wanted to be certain, though.

She wanted to see if he was still lurking somewhere. It was so weird; nothing could be taken as a coincidence nowadays. That's why she had rushed to call her lieutenant Ron before even beginning her meeting with Jose. Something just wasn't right.

"What the fuck is going on?" She said to herself, still with that gut feeling.

12

RICO

An hour earlier

"Hola, el Jefe," Rico started as he shook Jose's hand and sat at the table. "I'm happy to finally meet you in person. Now I can really put a face with the name."

They were both now sitting in the back of the coffee shop in an area that they usually used for the kitchen area.

"Rico," Jose began, "your proposition sounds very intriguing, but my question is more along the lines of loyalty. I have done business with the Andrews family for some time now. Why would I take on a new risk with new blood?"

Rico was prepared for this question… "If anything, I feel like if there's anybody that has put the work in out here amongst these streets, it's me. I've put my life on the line to see this family eat and run *The Network*."

"One may see this as jealousy, no?" Jose quickly added.

Rico was prepared for that, too… "Jealous? No. Ready to take *The Network* to the next level? Yes. There's a lot of potential and a lot of resources to be utilized, and we don't need to be wasting time waiting for Ceasar to get out. The Network can become obsolete in that time, and you know that."

Jose thought about it.

"Wow… nicely put, Senior. I hear you, and in due time, we all will see the true results of all our actions."

"Look, Jefe… all I ever wanted in my life was for someone to give me a chance. I'm not a snake, nor have I ever fucked someone over that has kept it one hundred with me. Ceaz has always looked out for me, which is why I wanna put an extra brick back for him each month when I come. I will charge extra on top of mine to make sure it's paid for," Rico promised.

Suddenly…

"I must say I never expected this. But OK, we can consider it done," said Jose.

"But look, this must stay between us for now," Rico told him. "I don't wanna have Diamond thinking that I'm on some slick type shit."

Jose assured him of this as the two of his bodyguards entered, passing Rico his own set of keys.

"Until we meet again, senior Rico."

Jose got up and disappeared into the back.

Rico chose to have his driver meet him out front,

which was unusual, seeing that he would never leave out of a door that he had entered through.

As he jumped into the back of the truck, he could feel his phone vibrating in his jacket pocket.

Ring

Ring

"Brotha, we just made it to the docks. We're just waiting for you," J.J. replied.

"Cool, I'm leaving Jefe now. Guess who the fuck I just saw pulling up to the spot when I was leaving?" Rico asked J.J.

"Who, Diamond?" He asked, already knowing what the odds would have been of Rico seeing her.

"Correctamundo. Clear as fucking day, bruh."

"Well, I'll be *fucking* damned. What's the play?" J.J. asked.

"She didn't see me, at least I don't think so. So that means ain't shit changed. We gone *take* her supply and make her think that it was them little niggas. After that, we should have the whole load to ourselves… then it's fuck *everybody*, nigga."

"Fuck it. Let's do this shit," J.J. told him.

But J.J. laughed as he parked and got into position, listening to more of Rico's bullshit ass orders.

"She should be on the way, two trucks deep at the most. Make sure it's a surprise party. Loud," instructed Rico.

"Say less," replied J.J. before ending the phone call, thinking to himself, "Something *big* is about to happen."

It was in the air.

13

CHASE

Outside the coffee shop

"Man, we been following this nigga for days," A-Wall stated as he dumped the tobacco guts from a *Swisher Sweet* that he was breakin' down. "I'm ready to pop sumn, bruh."

"Boy, shut yo ass up and roll that blunt. I would have been done deaded this nigga if you wouldn't have been pushing this hoe so fast," Chase barked, speaking of how fast A-Wall was driving at the mall when they first had the chance to kill Rico.

"Both of y'all shut the fuck up. Y'all niggas going back and forth like some lil females or sumn. Look, when this nigga comes out, we gone follow him til we on the highway… then flush him, and we out."

J.J. silenced both of the young guys while loading a Mac-11 subcompact machine pistol clip from the passenger seat.

"Watch this shit," he told them.

Pulling a phone from his jacket pocket, J.J. dialed Rico on speed dial.

Just as he hit 'send,' they could now see the usual black SUV that he would take when doing business.

"See, just like clockwork," said Chase from the backseat as he pointed out Rico exiting El Jefe's coffee shop.

Ring

Ring

"Brotha, we just made it to the docks. We're just waiting for you," J.J. replied.

"Cool, I'm leaving Jefe now. Guess who the fuck I just saw pulling up to the spot when I was leaving?" Rico asked J.J.

"Who, Diamond?" He asked, already knowing what the odds would have been of Rico seeing her.

"Correctamundo. Clear as fucking day, bruh."

"Well, I'll be *fucking* damn. What's the play?" J.J. asked.

"She didn't see me, at least I don't think so. So that means ain't shit changed. We gone *take* her supply and make her think that it was them little niggas. After that, we should have the whole load to ourselves… then it's fuck *everybody*, nigga."

"Fuck it. Let's do this shit," J.J. told him.

But J.J. had been planning his own coup...

The setup had been a plan the whole time, but Rico

thought that *he* was the mastermind.

"Aight… as soon as we pass the next overpass, we gone light that bitch up," J.J. told his crew after readying the fully loaded Mac-11 that was sitting on the floor between his two feet.

As they passed their mark, Chase and J.J. rolled down both of their windows just as they came up on Rico's rear passenger door. You could now see them both positioned in the windows of their car hanging over the roof.

Within seconds, there were bullets riddled all throughout Rico's black SUV. One by one, you could see bullets tearing pieces of metal from the truck and shattering windows.

The driver was struck in the temple and torso, causing him to lose control of the vehicle, veer off the road to the left, and crash out.

Skrrrrt…

The truck flew off the side of the freeway, missing the guard railings that would have kept it on the road. But they still would've never had a chance. There were bullets and debris everywhere.

"You think that nigga is dead?" A-Wall asked as J.J. and Chase stood on the ledge of the highway's shoulder with him, looking down at the flames that were billowing out of the flipped SUV now lying at the bottom of a hill.

"Shiidddd, Superman couldn't have survived that shit, bro. Now, come on," J.J. was telling his crew, "We gotta beat that bitch Diamond to the docks."

The trio hopped back in the car and fled the scene.

14

DIAMOND

Diamond had learned the game early on from Ceasar… *never leave any stone unturned.*

Something about seeing Rico coming out of Jose's place earlier truly bothered her. With El Jefe acting funny about their shipment, it started to stir up certain vibes within her.

It was one thing that he wanted to give her only a third of their usual full shipment, but to do business with Rico behind her back, if this is what he was doing, would definitely be an all-time low. This ranked at the bottom of the list of all the shitty things that Ceasar had always shared with her about Jose's funny ways at times.

Respectfully, she had expressed her loyalty to Jose in a way that she thought he would understand. But now, she was starting to get the feeling that he was playing both sides of *The Network*. She had to do some fast thinking.

Diamond's women's intuition was usually on point and led her to make better decisions when it came to being a few steps ahead of the game. But today, something about the game was fucked up, and things just weren't sitting well with her. But just as she was about to say, "fuck it," it dawned on her.

"Ron," Diamond said, speaking into her cell phone.

"Yes, Ma'am, Boss Lady…"

"Hey, do you still kick it with ol' girl that stayed across the street from Ceaz' plug.. the one that owns that coffee shop?"

"Who, Lisa's fine ass? Hell yeah. Every now and again. Why… wassup?"

"Call her for me and ask her if she got one of those *RING* doorbells that everybody has nowadays. The one that records shit all the way out to the street and shit?"

"No problem, boss. But if she does, what do you want me to do?"

"See if she can download everything that's been on it for the last past hour and a half and send it to you. But I need you to get right on top of that for me?"

"Say less," The dude told her.

Diamond was thinking of how much of a shot in the dark this idea was going to be, but again… it was that woman's intuition kicking in and speaking to her again.

If Ron was good, then his little female friend was even better. She actually did have one, and it turns out that the girl had dated a guy who must've worked for

Jose at some time, and she was still a little sweet on him.

The problem was the guy that she had dated was a player and always had girls stopping by the shop to see him… all the time.

Ron's friend had *two* cameras aimed at the place, and the clarity was so damn good that you could actually see the faces of every person who may have come and gone.

"Damn, was she obsessed or something with this dude?" Diamond asked after receiving her forwarded text message of the video.

She added, "Ron, make sure that you do something nice for this girl soon, okay? She might just have what we need in here."

Damn... and she did.

Nothing seemed out of place at first until…

Diamond didn't believe her ears!

The damn microphone on this thing had picked up audio all the way from the damn street!

Diamond questioned herself, "Was this girl listening in on all the guys' conversations with the other girls as well?"

"Shit!" She said to herself.

After noticing in the video a car sitting across the street from Jose's shop but diagonally from it, she recognized three male figures sitting in it.

The funny thing was… it was directly in front of ol girl's apartment, and the audio was impeccable.

Diamond recognized the voice and heard the whole damn conversation.

It was J.J., and she could hear everything... even the part where he was explaining to his little punk-ass crew how they were about to jack Rico... *AND HER!*

15

THE TWINS

The call to da hood

"Wazzam, D? Tell me sumn good, my girl."

Keon was just finishing up washing his car at the local car wash off of Martin L. King Boulevard.

This was a high-traffic area known for hustling, drug sales, and prostitution.

It had always been a dangerous and, according to some law officials, nuisance-like area for years, and only those accustomed to those types of lifestyles hung out there.

Keon was one of them… every time he visited the city.

"I need your help. Like right now, Kee," Diamond told him, adding, "You know I wouldn't even hit yo line up if it wasn't something serious. Things are starting to get a little crazy out here for real, Cuzo… and I need cha."

"D, I don't care what it is, you know I'm ridin' til the wheels fall off. That's actually the only reason why me and Dee are still here in Texas. I felt like you wasn't you the other night. So what's going on?"

"Square bidness. It's some mo' shit. But check this out..." Diamond began.

Diamond had devised a plan to not only keep the keys that Jose had provided for her earlier but also to get the fourth key as well. The fourth one was rightfully hers.

She and her team had put in all the work for it, and here, someone was... trying to take it away?

Thinking of all the events that had happened leading up until now, Diamond couldn't help but feel some type of way, but she knew that she still had a job to do.

"Kee, I'ma shoot you the address to that shop over there on Lamar. Let that be your starting point. I want you to follow the GPS route from that address all the way to the address at the pier, and when you see these little ass niggas... light that bitch up and keep that muthafucka on fire till I pull up. I know you remember how we used to throw parties for niggas who tried to run off with the bread?" And then Diamond answered her own question... "Yeah, that part."

Diamond had given Keon the description of the car that she had seen in the video from ol' girls' video footage. After seeing that the address that Diamond had sent to him was only five minutes away from where he currently was, Keon went into business mode.

But Diamond had another plan in mind as well. She was going to put a stop to all the bullshit that Jose had been pulling for years. Especially the part about him thinking that women were weak and couldn't run an organization any bigger than the size of that little bullshit-ass coffee shop that he had had her sitting in earlier.

"Is that the black car that Diamond shot us a video clip of?" One of the twins had asked his brother.

"Yeah, that's them, my boy."

"Why are they driving so damn slow?" He asked.

"Shidddd, if I'm not mistaken, it looks like they trying to trail that black truck further up ahead up there," Deon replied.

"What da fuck going on?... just play it cool," Keon said before adding, "Hey, fall back behind that Charger so we can watch how this shit is about to play out. You got dat *Draco* ready?"

As the twins fell back, they could now see the figure of a younger guy climbing out onto the window seal of the car with a gun, aiming at the truck.

"Whoa, Whoa, Whoa!!! What da fuck?" Deon shouted as he saw a total of two masked gunmen now unloading automatic weapons into the side and windows of the truck.

The twins weren't exactly confused. Shit, they had seen plenty of this type of shit before. But damn... they didn't know what to make of this shit right here.

All they knew was this... as soon as these niggas

who had just done the shooting at their target finished, it was going to be *their* time to fire *their* ass up.

They watched as the damaged truck started to swerve. Keon could now see debris and glass beginning to stretch all across the highway's pavement.

Just as Deon was bringing the car to a halt, they both could see the SUV fly over the side of the hill, just missing the guard rail.

Both of them also heard the crash. The truck then exploded into flames.

"Dammnnnnnn," the twins said to themselves.

Seeing the three guys get out of the car, they could now see the faces of the guys who had been doing all the shooting.

From the looks of everything, it seemed as if they had orders to carry out as if it was a hit or something.

But they still watched in amazement as the three guys walked over to the edge of the highway and stared downward at the crash with an air of victory about them.

Every one of them... and neither one of them seemed to even notice that somebody else was about to bring *Part II* to their asses... straight up *Boot style*.

They left the scene in a hurry... each fueled by hunger, each blinded by greed.

The twins had begun to go into a mode that they went into when it was time to become gremlins and wipe a nigga's nose.

Together their minds were preoccupied with

murder, money, and fucking over the one nigga who had tried to plot to get their cousin. Some niggas named J.J.

Keon looked over at Deon and dapped him up. Together, they said almost in a chant… "Family is everything… and fuck niggas ain't shit!"

The twins were ready.

But Chase, A-Wall, and J.J. had failed to reload by the time they saw the window of a car riding beside them come down.

"Fuck nigga!!" Kee screamed as he unloaded every bullet from his twin Glocks until both of their dicks were empty.

J.J. 'nem didn't know what the fuck was happening… and then they heard.

"Cat's out the bag, bitch!!!" The other twin yelled, shooting the *Draco*.

Deon was bussin' the *Draco* so hard at these muthafuckas that he damn near fell backward out the window.

"Damn," he said, sliding back into the car with a bounce on his seat and laughing, "Bro… I almost fell up out this muthafucka."

Keon asked him while he was digging another clip out from under his seat, "You good?"

"I'm good," Deon told him after sliding a couple more jars onto his *Draco*.

"Let's finish these niggas off."

Two of the guys were dead, but the twins just

couldn't believe that the *driver* was still alive and still maneuvering that big ass car around.

But he was looking at them… and they were looking at him, and each of them was starting to push their cars to top speed.

"Where you running to, you fuck nigga? Pull over and let me sing you a song, bitch!"

But J.J. wasn't having it… and he surely wasn't giving in without a fight.

"What the fuck? Who are these niggas?" He wondered.

But it really didn't even matter any longer. Chances were slim that he could just pull over and introduce himself… try to work some shit out or something.

"Fuck!" He screamed to himself, and then he turned to pay attention to the road and his driving as his car began to go into a curve.

J.J. could now see that the other car had slowed down. But why?

Had they run out of gas?

Bullets?

Nuts?

Had they changed their minds?

He realized that the answer to all of those questions was 'none of the above.'

Coming out of the other side of the curve, he saw what the deal was… A FUCKING ROADBLOCK.

Diamond and Ron somehow beat the odds *and* the traffic and met on the highway.

They knew the full route, and now here they were, blocking both lanes of the small two-lane highway with *ARs* pointed at the only figure that they had seen in the approaching vehicle.

Somewhere off the road in the middle of the woods

"D, I know what this shit might look like. But trust me, we were never going to fuck over *The Network,*" J.J. stated nervously.

"Man, save all that bullshit for somebody that wanna hear it, J.J.…. you see, the funny thing is, I actually used to tell Ceaz to bless yo game. *All* you lil niggas really. Now, look at you biting the hand that feeds you. *The Network* was built to give youngstas a chance to do something different. A chance to feel like you actually belonged to something. But look… see how niggas get greedy and fuck it all up? Man, I have been down with Ceasar and stayed down on Ceasar's side since the age of 16, and we built this organization brick by brick. I be *damned* if we lose it all behind some lil nigga who can't decide on what side of the fence he wants to be on."

"But, Dia…," J.J. started, but was hit mid-sentence dead in the mouth with the butt of the *AR* that Diamond was holding.

"Fuck!" J.J. yelled out and spat as blood began trickling from between his now swollen and aching lips.

"You know what?" Diamond said, checking to see if there was a round in the chamber of her gun. "Fuck this shit!"

"OK, OK, OK!" J.J. screamed.

He raised his hands in the air as Diamond took aim right between his eyes.

"That's right, nigga. Beg for your life like the little bitch you are. Chunk that shit up, lil nigga. Lift up yo muthafucking head!" Diamond said, making J.J. raise his chin and prepare himself to meet his destiny.

The tears were rolling down to the end of his face and dripping onto his shirt when he heard her ask…

"Do you have anything left that you wanna say, NIGGA?"

J.J. thought about it. Maybe there was a chance…

"Yeah, I do," he told her.

"So what, nigga. Fuck you!"

Pow!!!

The gun went off, sending waves of echoes all through the woods as no one even moved.

"Damn, D… I didn't even know you were really built like that," Deon told her, taking the gun out of her hand. "You really are a gangsta, huh?"

"Nah, cuzo," Diamond answered before turning to walk away.

But she stopped.

Diamond, now looking the twins square in the eyes, replied with only these simple few words as she thought of something that only Ceasar would say.

She told them, "Nah, cuz… I ain't just no gangsta. I'm a full gangsta and a half."

The End

www.ingramcontent.com/pod-product-compliance
Lightning Source LLC
Chambersburg PA
CBHW020527160726
47992CB00005BA/2280